THE BAKER'S BRIDE

The Romance Bride Series
Book 1

Cecelia Dowdy

This is the bread which cometh down from heaven, that a man may eat thereof, and not die.

—*John 6:5*

The Baker's Bride © 2023 Cecelia Dowdy
This novel is published by Divine Desserts Publishing LLC.
All rights reserved. No part of this book may be used or reproduced in any form or by any electronic or mechanical means, including information storage and retrieval systems, without written permission from the author.
This book is a work of fiction. Names, characters, businesses, organizations, places, events and incidents either are the product of the author's imagination or are used fictitiously. Any resemblance to actual persons, living or dead, events, or locales is entirely coincidental.

Printed in the United States of America.

For more information, or to book an event, contact :
cecelia@ceceliadowdy.com
http://www.ceceliadowdy.com

Cover design by Virginia McKevitt
ISBN - Paperback: 978-1-7338926-5-0

Dowdy writes with the right touch to keep the readers engaged and vested...
- **USA Today**

1

Philadelphia, Pennsylvania 1859

"Son, when are you going to get married?"

Oh no, she had to go and mention that. His mother acted as if he were the only unmarried, upper-class Negro man in Philadelphia. Joseph Adams ignored her and shoved the paddle into the hot, wood-fired masonry oven. He pulled out the thick, crusty loaves of bread. Thin fingers of sweat trickled down his face. He set the paddle of hot bread onto the counter and flexed his aching arms. The pain reminded him of his late-night excursion with other free black abolitionists. He'd been unloading supplies into the church, getting ready for the next group of runaway slaves they were expecting. The yeasty scent of the bread enveloped him as he sighed and wiped his forehead with a towel. Hopefully, his headache would go away soon.

"Boy, you hear me talking to you?"

"Mother, I hear you." Did she honestly think he could predict when he'd be getting married? His mother's mouth pressed down while she arranged loaves of bread into large square baskets. Her bony shoulders drooped. She'd been so miserable since Father died one month ago.

Joseph focused on the rough pine walls and two empty slab tables in their bakery. Visions of sitting with his father at those tables, talking about life, filled his mind. He eyed his mother. She hadn't been eating as well as she should be, and she'd lost a lot of weight. He was worried about her, but when he tried to get her to see the doctor, she'd get upset. He heard her crying every night. He hoped she'd soon heal from her sadness. He figured her grief was what was making her act so irrational about his future.

He pointed to the office in the back room. He

briefly eyed the stacks of parchment papers and inkwell resting on top of the antique desk and focused on the painting of his late father centered on the wall. "Didn't you tell me you had to do some bookkeeping today?" Maybe if he got her focused on something else, she'd stop asking him about holy matrimony.

She shook her head, the red kerchief on her head bouncing with the movement. "You never answered my question about marriage."

No, he hadn't. She'd asked that question at least ten times over the last month. His response hadn't changed, so why bother answering? "Mother, I don't want to talk about marriage." He again gestured toward the office. "If you don't want to do the bookkeeping, then why don't you go and rest for a bit." He figured she could sit in the chair and prop her feet up. Maybe close her eyes for a few minutes.

"No, if anybody should be resting, it should be you. You got up before I did." In spite of her words, she made her way to the office. She dropped into the chair and propped her feet onto a stool and leaned back. "You were up hours before I was." She closed her eyes.

Indeed he was. He missed having his father in the bakery, helping out in the kitchen.

Now he had to work even harder since they had yet to hire someone to take his father's place. Working the extra hours made him sick, literally. Thoughts of running away from the family business and never looking back rushed through his mind. How nice it would be to never bake another loaf of bread. The loud screech of the door opening invaded his thoughts.

Joseph focused on the small, dark-skinned woman who strolled into his shop. A few black curls peeked from beneath her bonnet. As soon as he spotted her full lips and sculpted cheek-bones, he paused. He could look at this woman all day. He took a deep breath, for he realized he'd stopped breathing. Her sharp eyes scanned the redbrick walls and rough wooden tables. He wiped his sweaty palms on his apron and approached her. "May I help you?"

"I's come about the job."

They'd just started looking for a replacement for his father. The few people who'd inquired had not passed his mother's approval. This was the first time they'd ever tried to hire a non–family member for their business. He cleared his throat and stared at the woman. Her skin was the color of the dark chocolate they sometimes used in their flaky, crescent-shaped croissants. He asked the first question that popped into his mind. "What's your name?"

"Ruth."

Ruth. The name suited her. He studied her warm, cocoa-brown skin and her cheap gray dress. Scuffed brown shoes covered her dainty feet. When he again focused on her face, she looked away, as if embarrassed.

Realizing his staring made her uncomfortable,

The Baker's Bride

Joseph glanced away and cleared his throat. He schooled his face to a stern, businesslike expression before shifting his gaze back to her. "Ruth, have you worked in a bakery before?"

"No, I—"

"Do you need my assistance, Joseph?" At Mother's voice, Joseph's stomach curled with dismay. Ever since his father died, Mother had watched his every move, as if she didn't trust him to run the bakery on his own. She focused on Ruth. "Did I hear you asking about the job?"

Ruth dipped her head. Mother scrutinized the young woman. "Yes'm. I's come to see about work."

Mother peered at her. "How did you know about this job?"

"Cyrus Brown says you lookin' for a baker."

Mother scrunched her eyebrows. "Who is Cyrus Brown?"

Ruth folded her arms over her chest. "He's an abolitionist over at the church."

"An abolitionist told you about this job?" Her voice vibrated through the room.

Joseph groaned inwardly. The last thing he needed was for Mother to get upset about the abolitionist movement. If she found out he was involved with the Underground Railroad, she'd have a conniption for sure. She'd often told him they should give money to the cause, but not get actively involved. He figured she was scared. She'd been so distressed since his father died that he had not found the right time to tell her about his recent involvement.

Mother cocked her head and squinted at Ruth. "How would an abolitionist know about this job?"

"Mother, it doesn't matter. Ruth is here now, so we need to consider her for the position."

Ruth nodded toward Joseph. "Thank you. I's glad you said that."

He gestured toward Mother. "Ruth, this is my mother, Elizabeth, and I'm Joseph Adams."

Ruth nodded at Joseph before focusing on his mother. She dipped her head. "Pleased to meet ya, ma'am."

Mother didn't acknowledge Ruth's greeting. Instead, her dark eyes assessed her like a hawk. "I can't have someone working in our bakery who talks like that."

Joseph cringed. He needed to step in, and Mother needed to tone down her elitist attitude. Their family had been free for two generations and had amassed a considerable amount of wealth. Mother wore their upper-class status like a badge, making sure everybody knew they owned their own business and catered to both white and black elite clientele. "She doesn't have to talk to anyone. I'll wait on the customers." As long as Ruth knew how to bake, he was sure she'd fit into their business.

Mother's chin jutted out. "I'm in charge around here. She just won't do."

The Baker's Bride

Ruth's dark eyes snapped to life, and she stood taller. She folded her thin arms over her chest and looked directly into Mother's face. "I's can bake bread better than anybody around here. Lets me prove it."

Mother stepped back, obviously stunned. Joseph smiled. People rarely stood up to his tall, overbearing, and outspoken mother. Joseph liked Ruth's spunk. Someone like Ruth was just what they needed around here to put Mother in her place. He needed to hurry up and give Ruth a chance before Mother got crazy and forced her to leave the bakery. He gestured toward their oven. "Come over to the oven, Ruth."

With quick steps, she followed him to the workspace behind the counter. She glanced at the dough trough, the wood-fired masonry oven, the large counter space. She then took note of the sacks of flour in the corner. She seemed to be taking everything in, an inventory of her new surroundings. "You gots any nuts, berries, dried fruit...cinnamon?"

Joseph opened the cabinet and removed dried cranberries, raisins, and a canister of cinnamon, pushed the items toward Ruth, then glanced at Mother and grinned. Mother remained uncharacteristically quiet. Usually when she met someone, she enjoyed dominating the conversation. Her silence told him she was either impressed or speechless—and it took a lot to make Mother speechless.

Ruth took the paddle, plunged it into the trough, and scooped some dough onto the counter. She then stopped and glanced around. "Do you have any dough that's already been set out to rise?"

"Yes." He rushed to give her the filled wooden bowl he'd placed near the oven earlier. She dumped the dough onto the workspace and sprinkled flour on top. Then, with deft hands, she worked the dough, sprinkling in the cinnamon, nuts, and dried fruit. Her small, delicate hands looked so lovely. . . He could imagine watching her knead dough all day. She stopped working, turning toward him. "Where's the other stuff?"

He frowned. What was she talking about? "Stuff?"

"To bake your bread. Sugar and stuff like that."

He pointed toward the cabinet. "I'll go get what you need."

She shook her head. "I'll get it." She opened the cabinet and studied the shelves. She removed containers, opened the tops, and sniffed each one. Their containers of spices were clearly labeled, so he figured she just wanted to make sure their spices were fresh. She stopped sniffing and looked directly at him. "Don't watch me." The command flew from her mouth as her dark eyes pierced his.

Goodness, he hadn't been expecting that. He focused on Mother. Her narrowed, dark eyes and pressed mouth indicated her building anger. Joseph's hopes for Ruth earning a position in their bakery deflated.

Not wanting to crowd Ruth, Joseph left her side and

strolled over to Mother, who gestured at Ruth as she leaned toward him. "Don't let that foolish girl give you orders. No way is she working here." Despite her whispered voice, he wondered if Ruth could hear her.

"Mother. . ." Joseph's grip on his temper slipped at Mother's imperious attitude.

He eyed Ruth again. It appeared she'd dumped some herbs and spices into a bowl. He wondered what she'd put into the dish. She dumped the contents into the dough and her hands again kneaded the mixture. Soon, she'd made four perfectly round small loaves. When she finally stood back and pressed her fists against her waist, he joined her behind the counter.

"I usually lets this rise for a hour. But I knows you don't want to wait."

Joseph figured Ruth knew Mother was uneasy about hiring her, and she wanted them to taste her bread as soon as possible. She took a pinch of flour and turned toward the large, beehive-shaped brick oven. Orange flames licked from the back of the baking hole. She tossed the flour into the oven. The cloud of flour floated down on the brick surface. The white powder slowly darkened from the heat. Her beautiful lips moved. He figured she was counting how long it took for the flour to brown. She then gave a little nod, took the handle of the large paddle, and shoved the loaves into the oven. Her lips continued to move silently. He wondered if she was counting, or praying. . .or what. She cleaned up her mess on the counter and returned the bowl to the cabinet.

A delicious fruity scent soon filled the kitchen. Joseph's mouth watered. He had been so busy he hadn't stopped for dinner that afternoon. The heavenly scent grew stronger, and Joseph's stomach rumbled. About twenty minutes later, Ruth lifted the paddle and quickly removed the hot, crusty loaves of bread. The dried fruit peeked through the cooked dough.

He opened the cabinet and removed the butter crock. They waited for the bread to cool slightly before Joseph sliced open one of the loaves. Steam exploded from the bread, releasing more of the delicious scent. He slathered butter on two thick slices of bread and carried the extra slice to Mother.

She eyed the delicious-smelling bread. Her eyes sparked with curiosity. She accepted the bread and took a hearty bite.

His stomach rumbled again as he bit into the bread. Heaven help him. This bread tasted amazing. The combination of fruit, nuts, and cinnamon exploded in his mouth. He closed his eyes. Melted butter dribbled down his chin. He gobbled another bite. He wiped the stray butter away with his hand. There was something else in this bread too. . . some other spices. . .what were they?

Mother gave him a critical glance. "Joseph, don't forget your manners. You're eating like a street beggar."

He stopped eating. Bristling at Mother's caustic

tone, he scowled at his outspoken parent. She'd eaten her entire slice of bread. He'd never seen her consume such a large slice of bread so quickly. It figured she berated him for eating too fast when she'd done the same thing.

Well, he didn't need to ask Mother if she wanted to hire Ruth. He already knew how she felt by the way she eyed Ruth's tasty bread sitting on the counter. Mother wanted another slice but was too proud to say so. He was taking matters into his own hands. He focused on Ruth, coaxing her into the corner. Mother hovered, but he didn't care. He needed to get Ruth to agree to work for them before another bakery snatched her up.

Her dark brown eyes appeared pensive and serious, and her pretty mouth drooped. Concern about being hired shone on her face. Well, she could stop worrying. Before he offered her the job, he had to ask her one question. "What did you put into the bread?"

She blinked, focusing on him. "I can't tell you."

He jerked back. "Why not?"

"That's my secret bread. If you want more of my bread, then you gots to hire me."

Well, he already knew some of the ingredients. . .so that was a start. But what if he wanted to make the bread? What if Ruth were sick or delayed from coming to the bakery? How would he manage to make this bread if she wouldn't tell him what was in it? Well, he'd figure all of that out later. For now, he just needed to make sure they hired Ruth. He offered his hand. "Ruth, would you like to work in our bakery?" He mentioned the wages they'd offer. Her pretty brown eyes widened. He wasn't sure if she was pleased or if she was upset because she wanted more money.

Her face split into a huge grin as she shook his hand. "Yes, I accept."

Mother narrowed her eyes. She approached them and pulled Joseph away from Ruth. "I need to talk to you."

He sighed and followed his mother into their office. He eyed the fountain pen, inkwell, and parchment papers that littered the desk. He wished Mother would focus solely on her bookkeeping duties and leave the hiring up to him. "Joseph, you can't hire that girl without my permission."

"I just did." It was high time he stood up to Mother.

"Well, you're paying her too much money." One reason their family had accumulated so much wealth was because Mother watched every penny they spent. She did the bookkeeping with a keen eye, always looking for ways to save money. "That girl is poor as they come. I can tell by the kind of clothes she's wearing. She's desperate for a job, and you could've offered her a much lower wage. She probably would've accepted it."

He shook his head. He didn't agree, not one bit. "Mother, Ruth is worth every cent I offered." He wasn't going to argue with his mother about this.

Sometimes, talking to her just made him so tired. He often wondered if she was so miserable she just wanted to argue for no reason. "I'm not a fool, Mother. You know just as much as I do that our customers will be lining up to purchase Ruth's bread."

"Well, let me tell you something, Joseph. That girl is here to bake and nothing else." She glared at him, folding her thin arms over her chest. "I saw you looking at her. If you even think about courting her, then you are a fool, the biggest fool I've ever seen in my entire life."

Joseph turned on his heel and stormed toward the door, knocking his knee against the desk. Pain shot through his joint as parchment papers scattered onto the floor. He had to get out of there. No way could he stay in Mother's presence for another minute. He limped toward the front of the bakery.

"Joseph, get back in here and pick up these papers."

The scent of Ruth's delicious bread lingered in the hot air. He pushed the door open and breathed deeply, limping outside and into the sun.

"Joseph!" his mother yelled from the door, but he'd already limped halfway down the
street. No way would she follow him. She wouldn't risk losing income by leaving the bakery unattended.

He finally dropped onto a bench beneath a huge oak tree. Bright sunlight sliced through the branches as the leaves danced in the wind. A man in a black suit rushed by, checking his pocket watch. Joseph closed his eyes and tilted his face toward the sky. He rubbed his aching knee and tried to calm down. He figured if he'd stayed around his mother another minute, he might have said something he'd later regret.

2

Ruth smiled as she scurried down Market Street. The strong scent of animals filled the air as horse-drawn wagons maneuvered down the road. She stopped, leaned against a tree, and closed her eyes. *Jesus, thank You so much! I's blessed to find this job!*

She opened her eyes and continued down the street at a slower pace. Folks in business suits rushed by, and a little boy stood at the corner, hawking candles.

Joy bubbled through her like boiling water; she just couldn't resist. She turned at the next corner and ran the last block toward the rooming house where she stayed. Miss Tilley, one of the boarders, unexpectedly came around the corner, and she ran right into her.

Miss Tilley's spectacles jerked to an angle, and she dropped her dinner pail and school satchel.

"Oh, I's so sorry." She rushed to help the schoolteacher gather her belongings.

"My goodness, Ruth, you were running like somebody was chasing you."

"I's sorry, Miss Tilley." She really wanted to be sure the schoolmarm was okay. "Anything I can do to help?" She handed the woman's dinner pail and satchel to her.

"Ruth, I'm fine. I just want to make sure you're okay."

"I's fine, delighted, actually."

"Well, glad to hear that. Why don't you come in and tell me why you're so happy? In the few days you've been here, I've never seen you look so delighted."

"I's be glad to tell you about it."

Miss Tilley opened the door to the rooming house, and Ruth followed her inside. The schoolmarm, the daughter of the elderly rooming house owner, looked at least ten years older than Ruth's eighteen years. She followed the older woman into the sitting room.

The sun beamed through the open drapes, highlighting the large pine table and chairs. A bookshelf nestled in the corner filled with several titles. Ruth ran her fingers over the spines. A longing to be able to read the words printed on the books' pages gushed through her. She pushed the longing aside as Miss Tilley went into the adjoining kitchen. She reappeared with a plate of sugar cookies. She placed them on the table and soon returned with two tin cups of water. "We can have ourselves a little snack. I'd told Ma I'd been craving some sugar cookies, so I'm glad to see that she baked some."

"I's can bake some good cookies. I don't mind doing that for you, but I's going to be busy working at the bakery." They settled into their chairs as she smiled and bit into a cookie. She enjoyed the delicious sweetness and took a sip of water, and then she told her friend about getting the job at Adams Bakery. "Miss Tilley, I's so glad to get this job. That's why I was running down the street. Not only is I glad, but I'm also worried."

Miss Tilley nodded, her wise, kind eyes focused on Ruth. "You mentioned you couldn't read the labels on the spices, so you sniffed them to see what they were?"

"Yes'm. Elizabeth. . .I mean, Mrs. Adams, didn't seem to like the way I talked. If she finds out I can't read, she might fire me."

Miss Tilley reached across the table and took her hand. "Honey, I doubt she'll fire you. From what you just told me, Joseph gobbled that bread as if it was the best bread he's ever tasted. I imagine customers will be flocking to Adams Bakery to buy your bread." She squeezed Ruth's hand. "That woman is as stingy as a miser. She watches her pennies, that's for sure. As soon as those profits start rolling in from your bread, there's no way she'll fire you."

"Really?" She wasn't so sure if money would be enough of an incentive for Elizabeth to keep her on staff.

"I can almost guarantee it. But if you want my advice, if I were you, I wouldn't tell her you're an illiterate former slave. If she ever asks you the question directly, then you can tell her, but otherwise, I'd keep that information to myself."

Ruth frowned. "Why? I's not scared of her." She sat up straighter in her chair. "I's not ashamed of being a former slave." She certainly didn't have control over where she was born and raised, so it was wrong of Mrs. Adams to hold her past against her.

"I've known both Elizabeth and Joseph for years. If she doesn't like someone, she'll make them miserable. For that matter, even people she does like, she makes miserable. That woman has been sad and upset for a while, and her negative attitude has gotten worse since her husband passed."

"Her husband died? That's so sad." Ruth mentally

sighed, able to relate to Mrs. Adams's pain. The woman was probably sad and needed some cheering up. Ruth needed to try to figure out what to do to make Elizabeth feel better.

"Yes, her husband's recent death is sad." The schoolteacher released Ruth's hand and gestured toward the bookcase. "I've noticed you looking at those books lately. I think it might help you working in the bakery if you learned to read and write. I could even teach you proper English, if you wish."

Ruth felt as if the schoolmarm had read her mind. On her journey home from the bakery, she'd wondered if learning to read, write, and speak properly would help with her transition to this new area.

After she'd been granted her freedom in her master's will, she'd been able to relocate from Maryland to Philadelphia. Arrangements had been made for her to have an abolitionist escort to her new home. In Philadelphia she'd become acquainted with Cyrus Brown, the abolitionist pastor at the local church. She'd only been there for a few days, and during that time, she'd found herself amazed and homesick at the same time. The city of Philadelphia proved far different from the huge Maryland farm where she'd lived her entire life. Seeing the tall brick buildings and crowds of people each day was still jarring. It would take her a while to get used to her new environment.

It was also an amazing shock to her system to see

blacks free, a few owning businesses, often walking down the streets unescorted. She certainly wasn't used to encountering a family like the Adamses, a black family with wealth. Just knowing a Negro could have money made her feel good inside, made her feel hopeful. Maybe there would come a time when all blacks were free. What a wonder that would be. *Lord, please help those still enslaved.*

Miss Tilley patted her arm. "Ruth? Are you all right? I asked if you'd like to learn to read, but it seemed you were daydreaming."

"I's sorry. Just thinking about my trip from Maryland." She dipped her head. "Yes'm. I'd like to learn to read."

She nodded. "Good decision. Learning to read will open your world up to so many things." She paused and took a sip of water. "I was also thinking you could help with the abolitionist movement. Both myself and my ma have been active for a while. Since you're a former slave, you might be interested in helping slaves to escape to freedom. The church I attend is a stop on the Underground Railroad. There's an abolitionist meeting there in a couple of days. After you return from the bakery, maybe we can have our first lesson and then go to the meeting."

"Me? Helping with the Underground Railroad?" She honestly couldn't imagine how she could help. What skills could she bring to the cause? All she could do was bake bread and cook an appetizing meal.

"Ruth, I can tell you're hesitant. But being a former slave yourself, I'm sure you realize how important it is for people to escape to freedom. Don't be scared. We pray before all of our meetings, and we feel led to do this."

Freedom! The feeling was so new to her that she was just getting used to it. The taste of freedom was so new and fresh, almost like tasting the sweetest nectar for the first time. She still wasn't used to not answering to her master. Her life had proved a whirlwind of change, and she didn't want to risk making wrong decisions. Feelings of inadequacy churned through her like sour butter. She'd been thinking of assisting with the Underground Railroad ever since she'd gained her freedom.

"But Miss Tilley, I's don't know what I can do to help. You's know I can't read. Can't write either."

"Harriet Tubman can't read or write. She's been wanted for years. She's the biggest advocate for the Underground Railroad. You don't need to be educated to help others." She patted her hand, stood, and gathered her dinner pail and satchel. "I've got to go and prepare my lessons for tomorrow. Just think about what I've said."

After they'd finished visiting, Ruth made her way outside to the small garden. Miss Tilley had shown her the herb garden, and she had volunteered to keep it thriving. The May sunshine enveloped the thriving plants with warmth.

She'd also planted some seeds that she'd brought up with her from Maryland. It'd probably be a week before they sprouted. She took a filled watering can and liberally sprinkled her seedlings and the other plants with water. She sniffed the aroma of rosemary, thyme, oregano, and other herbs. She used combinations of these herbs to give her bread a unique, distinctive taste.

Small paper sacks lined the edge of the garden. When she'd journeyed to Philadelphia, she'd brought bunches of her dried herbs with her. She opened a sack that held one of her unique combinations. She sniffed. Since she couldn't read, it wasn't possible to label the packs of herbs. Instead, she deduced the contents by sniffing. This sack contained her unique herb combination, which paired nicely with the cinnamon and raisins she'd used in the bread this morning. She'd hid the herbs in her satchel and was glad Joseph had done as she'd commanded and not watched her.

In due time, Joseph and his mother would figure out she snuck her own herbs in the bread. However, if she was discreet about it, she might hide her secret for a long while. She hoped to keep her secret as long as possible. After watering the plants, she went up to her room, looked out the window, and studied the street. A few couples walked together, holding hands. She studied the redbrick buildings surrounding her, still astounded that Philadelphia was now her home.

The supper hour was drawing near. The scent of

vegetables and meat drifted from the kitchen downstairs. Miss Tilley's mother had started supper. As she stared at a horse-drawn buggy clomping down the street, she again recalled her home.

She missed Maryland. No, she didn't miss not getting paid for her job, but she missed the other slaves, her friends, and the bit of camaraderie they'd shared. When she'd left, her departure had been bittersweet. Yes, memories filled her mind, some good and a lot bad. She squeezed her eyes shut, recalling how she'd lost the only man she'd ever truly loved. The death of the man she'd loved on an adjoining plantation still shook her to the core. She squeezed her hands into fists, her eyes still closed.

The pain from slavery ran deep, and she had to do what she could so that others didn't suffer too. Granted, her suffering was probably minor compared to what others had experienced, and were still experiencing, in their days of slavery. She leaned against the wall and wiped away the unwelcome tears from her eyes. She again recalled the abolitionist meeting to which Miss Tilley had invited her. Yes, she'd be going to that meeting. She'd do all she could to help abolish slavery.

3

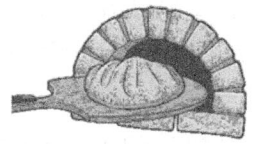

Joseph shoved the last bite of beef into his mouth and washed it down with water. "Joseph, stop eating so fast."

He needed to get to the abolitionist meeting tonight. No way was he telling Mother about that. He didn't want to be late. He would've skipped supper so he could get to the meeting on time, but he figured it would have aroused Mother's suspicions. They were having supper late that evening for a good reason.

Mother had gone over the accounting ledgers for the last couple of days. Since they'd hired Ruth, their profits had increased by 25 percent. Just seeing the increase of income in two days' time had somewhat pacified Mother about hiring her. She still barked at Ruth with a stark tone, but he figured in time, Mother would learn to treat her with the respect that she deserved. He certainly hoped so.

"I've got something to do tonight."

"What's that?" She narrowed her eyes and gave him a shrewd look. "Joseph, you better not be hiding anything from me."

"Mother, I'm a twenty-five-year-old man. Stop treating me like a child. I don't have to tell you everything I do."

She frowned and pushed her plate away. At least she'd finished half her supper, which was a blessing. Her appetite seemed to have returned since they'd gotten extra money into their coffers. "Are you going to call on Francine tonight?"

"No." The beautiful Francine was an upper-class black woman whom he'd escorted to one formal event. The woman proved whiny and clingy. One evening alone with her was enough for him to determine they did not belong together.

"Then where are you going?"

It was none of her business. He pushed his chair back, stood up, and kissed her cheek. "I'll see you later, Mother." Hopefully she'd be in bed by the time he returned. The last thing he needed was to have her subject him to an inquisition when he came home.

Ruth's hard shoes pounded on the cobbled street as she rushed to the abolitionist meeting. The last couple of days working in the bakery had been busy. She flexed her aching fingers. She'd never kneaded so much bread each day. When she'd been a slave on the big farm, she'd cooked, cleaned, and baked a few loaves of bread daily.

Working in a bakery was much different than kneading bread for farmers and workers. It'd been a blessing that she'd been able to keep up with the orders. People lined up down the street to purchase her herbal, cinnamon, dried-fruit bread. Joseph's hazel eyes had been laced with kindness when he'd seen her rushing to keep up with the orders. She'd been so tired, and he'd kindly offered to help bake the bread, but she didn't want him to know her secret recipe.

A young man rushed by so quickly, he bumped right into her. She blinked, and her steps faltered as the scent of male sweat—and corn—filled her nose. Thomas. This man smelled just like her deceased beau. "So sorry, miss." He bowed his head, and her heart skipped; his cinnamon-colored skin, tall, lanky frame, and deep voice reminded her so much of her beloved. He raised his head. His almond-colored eyes sparkled with warmth. She released the breath she'd been holding. Of course, it wasn't Thomas. The man gave her another smile and rushed away.

Salty wetness slid down her cheeks. She swiped the tears away. Thomas had been dead for over a year, yet that was the third time since his passing she'd imagined seeing him. The first two times had occurred while she was still living on the Maryland farm as a slave. How foolish could she be? Thomas had died, he'd been buried, and that was that. Slavery, that's what had killed Thomas. If he had not been a slave, she figured he'd still be alive.

The conditions of Thomas's death still haunted her. He'd lived on an adjoining farm and had taken ill. His master didn't send for the doctor, thinking he could treat Thomas himself. They concluded Thomas had contracted cholera. If the doctor had been summoned immediately, he might have lived. His death had hit her hard. She'd continued working in the kitchen as if in a trance. She couldn't eat, couldn't sleep. She'd been like a walking phantom, unable to fathom life without her beau. They'd discussed getting married, jumping the broom. She was about to approach her master about her intended plans just before Thomas died.

She continued to wipe her tears as she spotted the small, redbrick building of the church, where flocks of people entered. Ruth stopped, took a few steps back. She swallowed and took a deep breath, recalling the last time she'd been in a crowd so large. A slave who'd tried to escape an adjoining farm had been beaten. She'd witnessed the poor man being beaten so hard. He'd died a few days later.

"Ruth, are you all right?"

Her heart skipped when Joseph touched her shoulder and pressed a white handkerchief into her hand. She blinked and suddenly realized she'd been crying. She sniffed. Her nose was running too. She mashed her lips down, squeezed the handkerchief, and closed her eyes. She'd done so poorly. She only cried when she was alone. If she was careful, she could avoid tears in public. Well, the few times she'd spotted someone who resembled Thomas she'd lost control, unable to keep her emotions hidden until she was alone.

Now, Joseph had seen her cry. She certainly hoped he didn't think she'd be a weak, sniveling woman while working in the bakery. She considered herself a strong woman, and she didn't want Joseph to think otherwise. She took a deep breath and stood up taller. She needed to pull herself together. She had to focus on helping with the Underground Railroad and worry about her grief later.

"I's okay." She wiped her wet eyes and blew her nose. She figured she could clean Joseph's handkerchief and return it to him later. She tucked it into her battered reticule and again focused on the crowd of people entering the church.

"Why are you crying?"

"Slavery. Thinking about it makes me sad." She didn't want to tell him about the beating she'd witnessed, or about Thomas.

"So, you're here for the abolitionist meeting?"

She nodded. "Miss Tilley was supposed to come with me, but she's sick." Before the meeting, Miss Tilley was supposed to start teaching her the alphabet so she could learn to read. Before she'd left for the meeting, she'd stopped by her room and had seen the metal sick bucket beside her bed. Miss Tilley said she had a stomachache and couldn't attend the meeting. Her ma had been tending to her. Ruth had some dried mint leaves and had brewed them into a tea and given it to Miss Tilley's ma to give her. "Might help with her sick stomach," she'd advised.

She'd been disappointed she'd have to attend the meeting alone. She didn't realize Joseph was a part of the abolitionist cause. Strange that Miss Tilley had not mentioned this when she'd invited her to the meeting a couple of days ago. Her heart skipped as Joseph touched the small of her back and led her inside the church. Lanterns were lit and crowds of folks flocked to the hard wooden pews.

They took the last two spots on the back pew. She spotted some whites amidst the mostly Negro crowd.

Joseph touched her hand and gestured toward the group of whites. "Those are Quakers." He mentioned their names. "They've been working with the abolitionists for a long time, trying to stop slavery."

She nodded. This was the first time she'd ever seen whites and Negroes openly meeting together. She surveyed the church, studied the rough wooden cross in the front of the room. *Jesus, I really needs You right now. Please take my sadness away.* Seeing Joseph had been a somewhat welcome reprieve to her sadness. She discreetly studied him while they waited for the meeting to begin. She'd been relieved when he didn't ask her more questions as to why she'd been crying.

Joseph was probably one of the handsomest men she'd ever seen, besides Thomas. His skin was cinnamon-colored. His complexion reminded her of a loaf of lightly browned bread. He was tall, muscular, and hardworking. His curly hair was light, too, like the color of dust. The color of his eyes was captivating. His eyes weren't dark brown, like hers; they were light, like the skins of the hazelnuts she'd once chopped for a pie.

Over the last few days, she'd caught him staring at her. For some weird reason, she felt he could see deep into her soul. When they'd taken their dinner break, his mother had hovered, as if afraid to leave them alone to eat. She'd sensed he'd wanted to talk to her, ask her questions about herself. When his mother had left to deposit money in the bank, a couple of skinny street beggars had shown up. Joseph knew them by name and had given them a loaf of bread and some milk.

She figured the beggars knew when his mother wasn't around, they could come seeking food. Joseph had been so kind, asking them questions about their lives, and he'd encouraged them to come to church. The beggars had left by the time his mother returned. She'd been touched by his kindness. She'd been thinking about his interaction with the vagrants all day. She might as well ask him about it. "It was mighty kind of you to help the street beggars today."

He raised his thick eyebrows. "Those two have been coming around for a few years. I've been praying for them. I think you know Mother doesn't realize that I feed street beggars."

She nodded. "Would she be upset about a loaf of bread and some milk?" It'd be upsetting to know Joseph's mother would withhold food from someone for a few pennies of profit.

Surprisingly, Joseph chuckled. "Hard to say. She might not say anything initially, but since I do it every week, yes, I could see her objecting." He touched her hand, and her skin warmed. "I hope working with Mother doesn't bother you very much. She's always been controlling, but she's gotten much worse since

Father died."

Ruth nodded. "I's sorry to hear that. Miss Tilley told me your pa passed. Anything I can do to make your ma feel better?"

His mouth dropped open, and he appeared speechless. He then focused on her again. "Ruth, that is so nice of you to ask. I honestly don't know what could help Mother feel better except some prayers."

She nodded. That sounded like a good idea. She almost felt ashamed she'd not thought of praying on her own. "All right. I'll be praying for your ma and for you too. I figure it's hard on both of you, since your pa passed."

"Thank you." He tilted his head, studying her for a few seconds. "What about you, Ruth? Are your parents still alive?"

Since she never knew her parents, she didn't know how to answer.

"Everyone, time to start the meeting." Cyrus Brown rescued her from responding to Joseph's question. She figured he'd ask her about it again someday. But she'd rather wait until she'd been working at the bakery for a while before she shared something so personal with him.

Cyrus leaned on his cane as he made his way to the podium. She'd heard he was close to eighty years old. He'd even revealed his health was starting to decline.

Cyrus's kind eyes stared at the audience. "The Lord wants us to do all we can to abolish slavery. We've already helped so many slaves to escape, but we must help more." He bowed his head, and Ruth lowered hers and closed her eyes. She focused on Cyrus's words. "Dear Lord Jesus, please be with us tonight as we try our best to abolish slavery. Please let Your Holy Spirit be with us during this meeting." He paused for so long that Ruth peeked at the front of the room and spotted Cyrus wiping his eyes. She pressed her hands together and closed her eyes again. "Please be with all of the slaves who are on the run right now, Lord. Help them to find freedom. Amen."

"Amen," Ruth whispered.

Cyrus opened his mouth and his deep voice boomed throughout the church. The words of "Amazing Grace" rippled through the church as others joined in with the song. Ruth smiled, camaraderie and familiarity sweeping through her being. She sang along with the crowd, glad to hear her voice blended in well with the others. Joseph's strong voice also filled the room, and she stole another peek at him. They shared a smile when the song ended.

He touched her hand and liquid warmth spread through her. "Amazing Grace" was her favorite Christian song. Her master had allowed the slaves one hour of worship every Sunday. During that time, they sang hymns to the Lord. A few times, a traveling preacher had spoken to them.

Cyrus cleared his throat. "If it's the Lord's will, we're expecting some slaves to come through within the next two weeks."

Murmurs filled the room. Cyrus waited until the people had quieted before he continued to speak. "For those of you who are new to the movement, we have to provide meals, a bath, clothes, and shelter to the runaways." Ruth focused on Pastor Cyrus's words as he spoke about the movement, giving a summary of all the duties that were involved to keep the movement going. "We also need volunteers to provide encouragement, and we need to be sure we have plenty of supplies. . ." Ruth kept eyeing Joseph. He focused on Cyrus, leaning forward. He appeared spellbound by Cyrus's speech, and she realized Joseph seemed happier here, in church, then he'd ever appeared at the bakery.

She sniffed. Joseph smelled nice, like freshly baked bread and spices. The delicious scents of the bakery clung to him, making him that much more appealing.

"I also want to announce that I'll be stepping down as pastor. I'm getting old, and I don't know how much longer I'll be able to pastor this church."

Murmurs again rustled throughout the church. Cyrus closed the meeting with a word of prayer. Joseph then looked directly at her. "Ruth, would you excuse me for a minute?"

When Cyrus dismissed the meeting, Joseph raced toward the podium.

4

Joseph approached Cyrus. His brown, bald head shone under the light from the lanterns. Several people came toward Cyrus, but Joseph pulled the pastor aside. What he had to say could not wait.

"Reverend Brown, I'd like to be considered as a pastor for this church." As soon as Cyrus had made his announcement, excitement slipped through Joseph like a raging fire. Since he'd started coming to this new church, the sermons had moved him. He'd taken to reading the scriptures more often, and he'd also started memorizing passages.

He'd also been talking about scripture to the street beggars he fed each week. He often worried about the vagrants and had asked for Cyrus's advice when ministering to the homeless men.

"Joseph, I'm not surprised. I was hoping you'd say something."

His conversations with Cyrus about scripture, ministering, and the abolitionist movement were like nourishment to his parched soul. He craved being in this church the way a thirsty man craved water. He suddenly wondered if Cyrus had been secretly guiding him toward pastoring the church. But was he qualified? After all, he'd never even given a sermon. Cyrus clapped him on the shoulder. "Prepare a sermon for the church service in two weeks. I'll let the deacons know you are interested. We may need you to preach for a few weeks before they decide to allow you to be pastor." He cleared his throat. "I'll still be around to guide you if you're chosen as pastor."

Joseph opened his mouth, about to ask another question, but Cyrus shook his head. "Joseph, I have to get home. It's past my early bedtime and my knees hurt. We can talk about this some more later, but for now, that's what you need to do."

Joseph nodded as Cyrus leaned on his cane and made his way through the crowd. Several tried to stop him to speak, but he waved them away, apparently exhausted. Eager to share his news, he glanced at the pews and found Ruth in the back, patiently waiting. Ruth was easily the kindest, most patient woman he'd ever met. Any woman who could work with Mother and not lose her temper deserved a reward.

He quickly made his way over to her. "Thank you for waiting. Can I escort you home?"

He was rewarded by her bright smile. She quickly nodded. They exited the church and started down the cobblestone street. A horse-drawn carriage passed by as street lanterns spilled light into the semidark night. He eyed Ruth as they strolled down the street. Her bonnet was neatly tied, covering her dark curls. He ached to remove it and see her hair.

She'd kept her head covered with her bonnet while working in the bakery. They'd been so busy he'd not had a moment alone with her. Longing to see her outside of the confines of the bakery, without Mother's hovering, resonated within him. They could always use help with the movement, and he figured she might be willing to help him tomorrow.

"Ruth, tomorrow I have to go to the printers to pick up the pamphlets to distribute with some of the volunteers. Would you like to come with me? We could meet up with the rest of the volunteers and hand out the literature to people on the street, asking for their support for the movement."

Her pretty brow furrowed, as if she were worried. She chewed on her lower lip. "I be glad to do that, Joseph."

"Wonderful. We can go after I close the bakery tomorrow. Mother will be leaving right before closing because she has an errand to run. So, she won't bother us."

"Your ma don't know about your involvement in the Underground Railroad?"

He swallowed and shook his head. Ruth was a nice, honest woman, and he sensed he could trust her. "No, she doesn't." He sighed. "If she knew, she'd be extremely upset."

Ruth stopped walking and looked directly into his eyes. Her brown eyes sparkled beneath the lit lanterns. She clutched her reticule as if she were nervous. "Joseph, you should tell your ma about your involvement. Don't be scared of her. Besides, won't she eventually find out if you're passing out literature on the street?"

Not only was Ruth beautiful and honest, she was courageous. He figured she wouldn't keep something like this from Mother if she were in his position. "Philadelphia is a big city. I could probably do this for a long time before she found out."

"Why wait? Tell her now. Won't she be even

angrier if she finds out on her own?"

Ruth had a point, but he didn't want to tell Mother about his involvement yet. The time just wasn't right. He didn't want to hear her objections while he worked in the bakery every day. She already complained enough as it was. They continued walking, and he squeezed his hand into a fist. He ached to hold Ruth's hand, but he didn't know if it was a good idea. Sure, he thought about Ruth every night before going to bed, and he loved seeing her in the bakery. But he figured it was too soon to let her know of his attraction to her.

"Joseph, I thinks you making a big mistake, not telling your ma about your abolitionist involvement."

He didn't want to talk about Mother anymore. Just talking about his mother was ruining a perfect spring evening. It was time to change the topic. "So, Ruth, where did you learn to bake bread?"

Her pretty eyes widened for a second, and she hesitated. It almost appeared as if she didn't want to share this information with him. "I worked in the kitchen on a big farm for a long time. The owner died. I's then decided to work in a bakery instead."

He paused, noticing the tightness in her cheeks and her hands shaking slightly. She seemed suddenly nervous. He didn't want to scare her off with too many questions. He figured she'd tell him more about herself as they got to know each other better. They approached the rooming house. They slowly walked up the steps. "When you see Miss Tilley, tell her I hope she feels better."

She nodded. "I'll do that."

Thoughts of kissing her pretty lips rushed through his mind. He took a step back. He couldn't risk kissing her. He didn't know if it was the right thing to do, and he honestly didn't know if she'd welcome his attention. Instead, he touched her cheek. "Good night, Ruth."

"Good night, Joseph."

He stayed on the steps until she unlocked the door and entered the house.

Ruth removed her apron and eyed Joseph as he moved the ashes with a wooden stick, putting out the fire in the beehive-shaped oven. Gray smoke curled up from the baking hole as the flames died. She wiped the sweat from her brow. It'd been a long workday, and they'd sold many loaves of bread, just as they'd done the previous days. Her bread continued to be popular at the bakery, and she'd overheard customers asking Joseph questions about her.

When he'd walked her home the previous evening, her heart had skipped. When he dropped her off at the door, she wondered if he'd kiss her.

She was glad he hadn't. When she'd gone to bed last night, she'd dreamed about Thomas. Although she enjoyed the time she'd spent with Joseph, she doubted she'd ever get married. Thomas's death still haunted her. She still thought about the conversation she'd had with Miss Tilley. She found that her desire to help with the movement had grown in just a few days' time.

She wanted to help as many people as she could to find freedom. She also wanted to tell them about Jesus. She felt that was her calling in life. She honestly didn't think she was strong enough to fall in love again. She sensed just helping others in the movement was what she wanted to focus on. Being courted by a man was not something she wanted to do right now.

She sensed Joseph wanted to ask her questions about her background to find out more about her.

Once, his ma had caught him staring at her, and he'd looked away as if he were embarrassed. During the day Elizabeth hovered, her eyes narrowed like a hawk. Whenever Joseph was about to speak to her, Elizabeth would appear, almost as if she suspected Joseph's interest in Ruth. Well, the woman should learn to calm down and not spy on her son. Even though Joseph seemed as if he were interested in getting to know her better, she knew once he found out she was an illiterate former slave, he'd avoid her like the plague.

His mother had such a strong hold on him that Ruth wondered about them. She treated Joseph as if he were a child instead of a grown man—a handsome grown man with light brown skin and amazing eyes. She'd overheard some of the young, female patrons flirting with him when they came into the bakery. He'd always rebuffed their advances.

Another thing about Joseph that proved troubling. Except for yesterday evening, she never saw him smile. He was always frowning, and he bristled whenever his mother came around, as if he resented her presence. He baked bread almost mechanically, as if he had no choice.

He removed his apron and came toward her. "Are you ready, Ruth?"

She nodded. His ma had left about thirty minutes earlier, and it was time to go to the printers to fetch the literature. She was still eager to learn to read. It was kind of sad she was passing out literature and she didn't even know what it said. Miss Tilley promised they could start their lessons right before bed that evening. She squeezed her hands together, eagerly wanting to learn to read and possibly write. Imagine that, writing her own name!

Joseph held the door open and they stepped outside onto the sidewalk. The hot sun beat down on them as they started walking along the cobblestone street. Joseph reached for her hand.

She shook her head and took a few steps away from him. She wanted him to hold her hand, but didn't think it was a good idea to allow herself to become smitten with Joseph, not until he knew all of her secrets. His attention would never grow into a fruitful relationship, so it was probably best if she didn't encourage his attention.

"You don't want me to hold your hand?" The disappointment in his voice made her pause.

"We don't know each other very well, and. . ."

He shook his head. "We can discuss this later, Ruth. I'm sorry if I offended you." He took quick steps, and as sweat poured down Ruth's brow, she forced herself to quicken her pace to keep up with him. She struggled to walk so fast, and her foot caught on a loose brick and she stumbled. She cried out, and Joseph turned around and caught her. "Ruth, I'm so sorry."

His deep voice washed over her like cool water on a hot day. His strong arms wrapped around her like a glove, and he smelled nice, like freshly baked bread. She looked into his hazel eyes and couldn't think of what to say. Her tongue seemed glued to the roof of her mouth. She took a deep breath—she couldn't let Joseph make her feel so unsettled. She cleared her throat and finally found her voice as she stood upright. "You sure do walk fast. You wasn't walking this fast last night."

"I want to get to the printers before they close, and I'm eager to start handing out the literature. I didn't remember you probably would not be able to keep up with me." He shook his head for a few seconds. "Accept my apologies, please. I should have been more considerate."

She didn't trust herself to speak. Her attraction to Joseph was as real as the sun shining from the blue sky. She figured her attraction would go away. She'd just been irritable from the heat, and she'd been afraid of falling on the street. Flustered, that was the way she'd been feeling, and Joseph's rescue had made her feel a bit better. "I's okay." He really did seem to feel bad about his mishap.

He slowed his pace, and soon she was strolling beside him. She almost stumbled again, but he quickly touched the small of her back, breaking her fall. "They need to replace some of these cobblestones."

Finally, they walked at a leisurely pace. The late afternoon sun shone on them with warmth. Ruth wiped her brow. "Sure is hot out here."

"Yes, it is hotter than normal today." He continued walking slowly, his feet clomping against the street. She had a lot of questions she wanted to ask him, but she wasn't sure if her curiosity would encourage him to ask more questions about her background.

"Ruth?" His deep, sultry voice interrupted their silent walk.

"Yes?" Looked like he had something he wanted to ask her too.

"You said we don't know each other very well. That's true. We haven't really had time to get to know one another since Mother is always watching us."

That was an understatement. She figured since they

were working together every day, it'd make sense to know something about one another. She gulped as they turned a corner. A horse-drawn carriage clomped down the street as folks rushed by. Hopefully, he didn't want to get too personal. She wasn't ready to tell him everything about herself. She figured it might be best to focus on him. "You mind talking about your pa?"

He frowned.

She touched his arm. "I sorry. I understand if you don't wants to talk about him."

He patted her shoulder. "I don't mind telling you about him. I was close to Father. He taught me so many things. I enjoyed working with him, more so than Mother. My father was the most honorable man I've ever known. I miss him."

She squeezed his arm. "Thanks for telling me." She wasn't sure why she wanted to know more about Joseph's relationship with his father. Perhaps she wanted to understand his relationship to his kin because she'd never had contact with many of her blood relatives.

The printers was just down the street. She wanted to ask her question before they arrived. "I have another question for you, Joseph."

He focused on her with his amazing eyes. "Really? What's that?"

"Why you so unhappy at the bakery? You seem happier when you're not there."

"If I had to explain, it would take me all day." He took a deep breath and looked directly into her eyes. "I hate working in the bakery."

Her eyes widened at his blunt statement. "Do your ma know?"

He shook his head, the tortured look returning to his handsome face. "I'm sure she suspects. A mother should know her own child, right?"

She shrugged. She'd never known her own mother, so it was hard for her to comment. "Why do you stay? Can you work someplace else?"

He dropped onto a nearby bench, and she sat beside him. She wanted to be Joseph's friend, and she hoped he'd feel comfortable confiding in her eventually. She honestly did not know what else to say. Just to be able to work and get paid was a new experience for her. She couldn't imagine not liking any job if you were paid.

He took a deep breath. "My family has been free for two generations. This bakery has been in my family for a long time. It's just expected that I work there and make my living, but I'm miserable. Mother's attitude makes it worse."

Ruth couldn't understand. After all, she loved baking bread. She felt at home in the kitchen and couldn't imagine doing anything else for a living. "Well, what would you do if you's could choose?"

"I have plans to do something else, Lord willing." He paused and peered directly into her eyes. "Ruth, I didn't get a chance to tell you last night. You know I went to talk to Cyrus after he announced his retirement?"

She nodded.

"I want to be considered for the position."

"You's leaving the bakery?" She couldn't keep the shocked tone out of her voice. If his ma found out, she'd have a huge fit. Ruth imagined his ma would make her life even more miserable if Joseph were not around. If Joseph became pastor of the church, Ruth figured she might have to find another bakery to hire her. She sure didn't want to endure Mrs. Adams's sour treatment if she could find the same wages elsewhere.

But if Joseph was called to be a pastor, who was she to judge? She recalled his kindness toward the beggars. She sensed he enjoyed ministering to others, so she needed to have faith things would work themselves out if he was appointed pastor.

"If I get the position, then yes, I'd be leaving. Mother will be disappointed."

She sure would be. Ruth didn't want to be anywhere near the bakery when Joseph told his ma his news. She didn't want him to get the wrong idea about her reaction. "I's happy for you, Joseph. I hope you gets appointed."

He smiled; his hazel eyes sparkled with warmth. "Thank you, Ruth. That means a lot to me."

He jerked his thumb toward the printers down the street. "We need to pick up the literature before they close."

She scampered to keep up with him as he rushed to the printers.

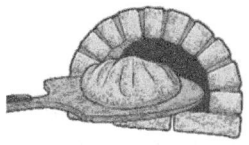

Ruth offered the literature to a well-dressed man. "Help stop slavery." She said a silent prayer of thanks when he accepted the paper.

"Help stop slavery." Joseph handed the literature to another passerby. The woman balled it up into a wad and threw it on the street. She glared at them before hurrying by.

Ruth had gotten used to the mixed reactions of the crowd as they'd handed out literature. After they'd gotten their leaflets from the printers, they'd met up with the group of abolitionists she'd met at church the previous night. Standing beside Joseph, hearing his deep voice as he offered the leaflets to the passersby. . .she felt his passion. Pride, that's what she felt. She felt proud to stand here beside him and hand out the literature.

"Joseph!" The high-pitched female voice rocked Ruth's core. She eyed the woman who sauntered toward Joseph. The lady wore an expensive frock and polished, buttoned shoes. Her skin was the color of a lightly browned loaf of bread, toasty. She carried a black umbrella to shield her pretty face from the sun. By far, she was the most beautiful Negro woman Ruth had ever seen. Her entire appearance screamed money, wealth. . . Ruth figured this gal was part of one of the elite black families in the area.

The woman fingered Joseph's lapel, her eyes downcast. "Why have you not called on me?"

Ruth's heart skipped a beat, and she was glad she hadn't allowed Joseph to hold her hand earlier.

"Francine. . ." Frustration and. . .something else tinged Joseph's deep voice.

Try as she might, Ruth just couldn't stop staring at this beautiful Negro woman. Joseph's crestfallen expression also had her enthralled.

5

Joseph narrowed his eyes. *Lord, please help me not to lose my temper.* "Francine, what on earth are you doing here?" Her perfume clung to his nostrils like an annoying ant. He took a few steps away from her.

She batted her eyelashes. "I came to see you. Joseph, you have not come to call on me since you took me to the cotillion a month ago. I just wanted to see you."

He'd never in his entire lifetime encountered such a bold and beautiful woman. Francine may have been beautiful, but her beauty was outward. He just couldn't warm up to her. A few weeks before he'd escorted her to the cotillion, she'd spotted him feeding the beggars as she rode by in her carriage. He had not realized she'd noticed his actions until she'd boldly confronted him about it on their way to the ball.

"I can't believe you'd feed those people, Joseph. Your mother told me you already give to the Philadelphia charities. You don't want those people in your bakery."

At that time, he'd hauntingly realized Francine sounded just like Mother. He didn't even want to ruin his day thinking about the abhorrent time he'd had at the cotillion.

"Joseph?" Her voice rose, just a bit, as she fingered his shirt. "Why aren't you speaking to me?"

He eyed Ruth as she continued to pass out pamphlets. She appeared busy, her bonnet covering her dark curls. She glanced his way for a few moments before continuing her chore. Her pretty mouth appeared pinched. Perhaps she was upset about Francine's unexpected arrival. Hopefully Francine would be on her way so they could return to their duties. "Francine, I've been busy." He showed her the pamphlets in his hand. "I'm in the middle of my abolitionist duties." He took a deep breath. "Listen, don't you want to abolish slavery?"

She narrowed her eyes before boldly offering her parasol. "Hold this for me, please." Another trait of hers that proved bothersome—she commanded him as if he were her personal worker. He swallowed and grasped the handle of her parasol. She then opened her fancy black reticule and removed a folded object. She opened her rose-decorated fan and waved it in front of her face in quick movements. She then accepted her umbrella. "It's hot out here today."

"Perhaps you should go back into your carriage." He was determined to get back to his duties, and having Francine around was not helping with his mission.

She narrowed her eyes. "Does your mother know about your involvement with the abolitionists?" It was no surprise she refused to answer his question about slavery.

He certainly could not lie to Francine, yet Mother's knowledge was none of Francine's concern. He'd tell Mother when he was ready. "I don't want to talk about her now. I'm busy."

She pursed her red-painted lips and again fingered his collar. "Well, the charity ball is coming up. . ."

He resisted the urge to groan. The charity ball. Mother had been hinting about the event for the past week, openly wondering why he'd not yet asked to escort Francine. Well, one evening of Francine's company was enough to last him a lifetime. No way was he going to ask to be her escort. He couldn't be rude to her, so it would probably be best if she left before he said something he'd regret. He gestured toward her carriage. "I don't want to make you late, Francine. It appears you were on your way to an engagement. I will speak with you another time."

He then turned to the next passerby, his back turned toward Francine. He supposed he should help her up into the carriage, but she'd already fingered his shirt twice and openly flirted with him. He recoiled from the notion of giving her yet another opportunity to flirt. As he handed a pamphlet to the dark-suited gentleman, he caught Ruth's open stare.

Over the next few days, the pretty woman Ruth had spotted on the street haunted her mind. Francine. That's what Joseph had called her. Since the day they'd handed out the pamphlets, Ruth had spotted Francine twice. She'd brazenly come into the bakery, bothering Joseph as he waited on customers. His mother enjoyed Francine's impromptu visits. The two of them had spent a full half hour in his mother's office. She had even asked Ruth to bring back a pot of hot tea and slices of her cinnamon, fruit bread with butter.

She'd overheard Francine's praises for the bread through the closed door. His mother had laughed, stating they'd hired a new girl. She'd also made it seem as if Joseph's business acumen had made their bakery even more successful.

She'd wanted to step into Mrs. Adams's office and tell Francine that she had helped make their business more successful, and she was most likely the best bread baker in all of Philadelphia. She gritted her teeth as she overhead their chatter behind the closed door. Joseph's ma still thought of her as nothing more than a hired hand—she didn't seem to want to acknowledge the talents she'd contributed to the bakery.

Well, there was nothing she could do about that. *Lord, help me with my anger.* She was here to do a job, and she continued to be grateful for her employment. She didn't need to think about Mrs. Adams's chatter right now. She had some more bread to bake. As she kneaded dough, she thought about the dream she'd had the previous night.

In her dream, Thomas had been stumbling in the darkness, blind, unable to see her standing right in front of him. She'd screamed, tried to get his attention. Joseph had stood in the distance, studying her with his intense hazel eyes. Francine had screamed at Joseph, but he'd ignored Francine's tirade. She'd awakened from the dream, stunned and confused. She'd been so upset she'd had to drink a cup of lavender tea to calm her nerves. She'd finally managed to fall back to sleep.

She ached to ask Joseph the nature of his relationship with Francine. He was cordial toward Francine. But it was hard to tell if he was smitten with the beautiful young woman. Thoughts about Francine and Joseph twirled through her mind like windblown seeds as she approached the rooming house after work. Miss Tilley occupied one of the kitchen chairs. She nibbled on a cookie while sipping a glass of water.

"What's wrong, Ruth? You look like you're about to cry."

She'd been so emotional since she'd come to Philadelphia. She'd been finding it hard to keep her emotions hidden until she was alone. "Nothing."

Miss Tilley patted the empty chair beside her. "Come on and sit down. We have a few minutes to visit before we start your lesson."

She'd been having a lesson every night since the schoolmarm had recovered from her stomach illness. Ruth had started looking at the newspaper. No, she could not read it, but she knew the first letters to some of the words. Oftentimes, she caught herself listening to customers while they talked. When she heard words, she found herself trying to figure out the first letter of the word. She'd been surprised when Miss Tilley told her that cinnamon started with a c not an s, as Ruth had assumed. She still had a lot to learn, and she was grateful the Lord had placed Miss Tilley in her path to teach her how to read.

She pulled out a chair and selected a cookie. Gingersnap, one of her favorites. She consumed the entire spicy cookie and enjoyed a sip of water. She'd not spoken of her weird feelings about Joseph to anyone. But she needed someone to talk to, and Miss Tilley seemed like she wanted to help. She took another sip of water before gathering her thoughts. "I's... I—" She paused. Miss Tilley had been teaching her the proper way to speak. She'd been trying hard to say I instead of I's. Sometimes she forgot, but she figured with enough patience and tutoring from Miss Tilley, she'd soon read and speak properly. Maybe Mrs. Adams would then feel comfortable enough for her to wait on the customers.

"I...am confused."

"Confused? About what?"

She told Miss Tilley about her dream the previous night and about how her heart thudded whenever Joseph was around. She spoke of Francine and about how her interaction with Joseph made her feel uncomfortable. "He is so handsome and strong. Plus, he cares about helping to end slavery."

Miss Tilley smiled and took her hand. "Ruth, there's nothing to be confused about. You're obviously sweet on Joseph. There's nothing wrong with that. He's good-looking, charming, and nice as can be." She cleared her throat. "Are you upset because he's not smitten with you?"

"Miss Tilley, my problem is, I just can't get him off my mind. But I needs to. I'm not supposed to be with anybody."

Miss Tilley frowned and pushed her tin cup aside. "What do you mean?"

"God called me to help people escape from slavery. I's. . . I feel the Lord led me here to help people escape through the Underground Railroad."

"Dear, I don't understand why that's a problem. You are helping with the abolitionist movement. So is Joseph. I'd imagine that would make him a perfect beau for you; that is, if he shares your feelings."

She shook her head. Miss Tilley just didn't understand. Not at all. "I'm not supposed to be with anybody. I'm spending the rest of my life alone, without a husband or children." She squeezed the older woman's hand. "I'm supposed to help men, women, children escape from slavery. I'm going to spend my life helping other people. Alone. That's what the Lord wants me to do."

"Oh, Ruth." Miss Tilley's kind, thoughtful voice filled the kitchen. Her eyes shone with curiosity, and something else that Ruth couldn't quite put her finger on. "Why do you honestly feel the Lord has called you to be alone your entire life?"

"Well, I's. . . I was going to jump the broom back in Maryland to Thomas."

"Thomas?"

"My beau in Maryland."

"What happened?"

Her eyes teared and she wiped the wetness away, unable to hide her pain. "He died, Miss Tilley. He lived on a nearby plantation. He got sick. His master didn't call the doctor soon enough. If he had not been a slave, I think his master would have called the doctor and gotten him the help he needed. Slavery killed the only man I ever wanted to marry. He been dead for eighteen months now. I still think about him every day."

"Ruth, I want you to do something for me."

"What?"

"Pray about it. You're still not over Thomas, but that doesn't mean you should remain unmarried for your entire life. Our lives are full of seasons, and maybe you are called to be unmarried, but maybe the Lord wants you to be unmarried for *now*. After you're over Thomas, maybe the Lord will see fit to open your heart to a man's love."

"I just don't know, Miss Tilley."

"Honey, listen to me. Listen to your heart. You like spending time with Joseph. Maybe being with him is part of the process of healing, learning to cope with your pain from losing Thomas."

Ruth continued to think about Miss Tilley's advice while she opened her primer to start her next lesson.

6

P salms, Proverbs, Ecclesiastes. . .Matthew, Mark, Luke, John. So many books of the Bible. Joseph flipped through it, staring at the pages. He leaned back against his chair, eyeing the stacks of parchment papers littering Mother's mahogany desk. Since she was out on an errand, he'd taken liberties and was using her office for the afternoon. Ruth had agreed to come fetch him if any customers came into the bakery. He continued to work on his sermon to present himself as a candidate for pastorship. He wasn't sure which verses he wanted to use.

He was still unclear about his message. He'd been praying to the Lord, seeking His guidance, as he prepared the very first sermon of his entire life. He wrote a few notes down on the paper. He needed some ideas, quickly. Time was running out, and he wanted to be sure he gave a sermon that would please Jesus, as well as the congregation. *Oh Lord, please help me.*

He rubbed his tired eyes. He'd been up late the previous night, reading his Bible and praying. Thankfully Mother had slept soundly and did not know he'd been up half the night. He sighed and patted his full stomach. He'd just consumed his dinner of fried chicken, a hard-boiled egg, two crisp apples, and several slices of Ruth's cinnamon and dried-fruit bread. She'd just slid several loaves into the oven before he'd entered Mother's office. The delicious scent filled the air with decadent sweetness. He'd been watching Ruth, still wondering how she made her wonderful bread. She shooed him out of the kitchen whenever she baked her loaves, and he longed for the day when she trusted him enough to tell him her secret recipe.

Secrets.

Ruth was full of them. He longed to take her into his arms and kiss her sweet, rosebud-shaped mouth. Her dark cocoa skin looked lovely beneath the sun shining through the bakery windows. He sensed a wall between them, a barrier. He'd caught her openly staring at him a few times. He was unclear as to if she was merely curious about him or if she had something else on her mind.

He'd wanted to find out more about her, but she'd been strangely quiet when he asked too many questions. Her responses had been vague, and he was unclear as to if his questions made her uncomfortable or if she truly did not enjoy talking to him. He supposed she may feel uncomfortable because of Francine's visits. The woman proved a bothersome thorn in his side, and he hoped Ruth did not mistakenly think Francine was his sweetheart.

He sniffed again. He could use a few more slices of bread. . . Bread! That was it! He plopped back into the chair. Bread—that would be the subject of his sermon. Spiritual bread. He opened his Bible and flipped through the pages. He scribbled, writing and mumbling to himself. He recalled which scriptures mentioned bread. He dipped his pen into the inkwell then scribbled some more. A loud knock broke his concentration. It couldn't be Mother. She'd never knock. It had to be Ruth. He figured she needed his help with some customers. "Come in."

Ruth opened the door. Her dark eyes settled on him. She looked lovely. Apparently, she'd gotten a new bonnet. Her head covering was bright red, and it contrasted nicely with her dark hair and mahogany skin. "You's... You said to remind you to stop...stop working when the bread was done."

He'd noticed Ruth had been doing that a lot lately, correcting her speech. He figured she'd found someone to teach her proper English. She probably was learning how to speak so she could be even more of an asset to their bakery. After all, if she spoke properly, then Mother would let her wait on the customers.

"Yes, that I did." He stood up. Mother said she'd be gone for an hour. He figured he'd have ample time to put his work away before she caught him working on his sermon. He'd made some good progress during her absence. He pulled out his pocket watch and checked the time. He still had fifteen minutes before Mother returned. Ruth bobbed her head once and turned away, as if to return to her duties up front. "Don't leave yet."

She slowly turned back around. "Yes, Joseph?" Her voice, sweet as honey, washed upon him like a river. During the workday, she seldom spoke unless he asked her something directly. She seemed more comfortable talking to him when they were away from the bakery. He certainly understood how intimidating it could be, trying to have a conversation with Mother hovering nearby.

The Baker's Bride

"You've been working here for two weeks. It's payday."

Her pretty dark eyes rounded, and she raised her becoming eyebrows. "Payday?" Before Mother had gone to bed the previous night, she'd finished reviewing the ledgers for the last two weeks. Their profits had increased so much from Ruth's bread that she grudgingly agreed to let Ruth have a few cents extra per day as a bonus. He was amazed he'd been able to convince his miserly mother to do this. But Ruth deserved it. Folks had been lining up in front of their bakery in the early morning for the last fourteen days to purchase Ruth's bread. Mother had been humming about the increased profits, and he'd had to gently remind her last night that Ruth was the sole person responsible for their increased profits.

If Ruth chose to leave, then their profits would decline. He doubted Mother wanted that to happen.

"Yes, it's payday." He had not discussed when she'd get paid when they originally hired her. He knew she was staying at Tilley's Rooming House, so he figured she owed for her room and board. He opened the drawer and pulled out a small sack. He quickly counted out her wages and approached her. He pressed the money into her small, flour-stained hands.

Her lips quivered as she counted out the cash. "But Joseph—"

"There's extra in there for your bonus."

Her eyes shimmered. She was going to cry? He'd

thought she'd be excited about the extra funds. "Thank you." Clutching the money in her fist, she leaned toward him and pulled him into a hug.

She smelled lovely, like cinnamon and spices. His heart pounded as he returned her hug; her delicate body fit into his arms perfectly. He now realized she cried tears of joy.

"I's. . . I'm going to take the bonus money and give it to the abolitionists. I want to do all I can to stop slavery." She gave him a little nod again and swiped her tears away before rushing back into the bakery.

He blew on his papers and made sure the ink was dry before he folded them into a neat square and shoved them into his pocket. He then made his way back into the bakery and stole a look at Ruth, who placed the freshly baked bread into baskets.

She was a strong, beautiful woman. Prayerfully, if he was patient, she just might agree to court him.

Ruth sighed as Joseph dropped into the empty seat beside her. The oil lamps glowed in the crowded room as Cyrus Brown took the podium. He cleared his throat before speaking. "The runaway slaves should be here in less than a week. We've been making all kinds of preparations. We have the supplies on hand, and we figure we will be hiding them underneath the church for a few days before we help them to the next station." He paused for a few seconds. "We also want to be sure we give the runaways ample provisions to take with them when they go to the next station. We've been making sure we have plenty of dried meat, bread, and potatoes for them to take with them on their journey." He continued to state what they needed to provide.

Her heart swelled. She hoped and prayed the runaways made it here. *Oh Lord, please help the runaways to find freedom. Please let them escape from slavery.* As Cyrus Brown continued to speak about their preparations, she recalled the funds she'd made from working at the bakery.

Joseph had paid her a few days ago, and she still found it hard to believe she'd actually earned her own money. When she'd first received the money, she stayed up half the night, thinking about her funds. She found a loose floorboard and placed her money in her hiding place. Her heart swelled as gladness filled it. This was the very first time she'd ever been paid.

Joseph shifted in his seat, making the pew creak beneath his weight. He looked tired. He'd mentioned to her during their dinner break that he'd been up late the previous night working on his sermon. Far as she knew, his mother still didn't know about his involvement in the abolitionist movement or about his wanting to be a pastor. Well, he needed to have a backbone and tell his mother. Sure, she'd be upset, but why keep it a secret?

Thankfully, she had not seen Francine in the bakery over the last couple of days. She still wondered about the bothersome woman. She'd caught Joseph watching her all day. She sensed something was on his mind. Well, one thing that had been on her mind was that hug. She could not believe she'd hugged Joseph when he'd paid her wages. His arms had felt big and strong around her. Being held by him made her feel safe, just for a few moments. His large, muscular build, light brown skin, and hazel eyes. . . She pushed those unwelcome thoughts away. *Lord, I'm sure attracted to Joseph, but, there's nothing I can do about it.*

Thomas still hovered in her mind. His death still haunted her dreams, and she recalled how he kissed her when he'd asked for her to jump the broom. Well, she couldn't focus on that right now. She just needed to be sure she was ready when the runaways came. That was all she was concerned with right now.

"I'd like to close with a word of prayer," Cyrus announced from the podium. She bowed her head, and her heart skipped when Joseph took her hand. Her hand felt warm and protected in Joseph's large palm. As Cyrus prayed over the runaways, she took deep breaths and listened to every word that came out of the pastor's mouth. He ended the prayer, and she and Joseph joined in with their amens.

She stood up and took a deep breath. Joseph stood

up beside her. He focused on her, his hazel eyes serious. "Ruth, can I—"

"Ruth. Joseph." Cyrus ambled over with his walking stick. "I wanted to talk to the two of you." He cleared his throat. "Joseph, since you want to be considered for the pastorship, I think it's best if you be there when the runaways arrive. You can help minister to them. I'll come and find you as soon as they get here. Do you know your whereabouts over the next few days?"

Joseph nodded. "Pastor, I'll either be in the bakery or at my home. I doubt I'll be elsewhere."

Cyrus focused on Ruth. "What about you, Ruth?"

"Me, Pastor?"

"Yes. I figure we should find you too. I think you should help minister to the runaways. I've received word that they'll often have to forage for herbs when they're on the run. I've heard you have a passion for drying herbs and cooking with them. Do you have some dried herbs to spare for the runaways?"

"Oh, Pastor." Her heart swelled. "Yes." She mentally thought about all of the herbs she'd dried. Miss Tilley's herb garden was thriving, so she could easily dry more herbs to replace what she'd donate to the runaways.

Joseph frowned. "I didn't realize they'd need herbs."

She turned toward Joseph. She'd need to explain this to him. "Yes. They's. . . They need them to help them to be healthy. They can also provide some nourishment." She went on to explain that echinacea could help them not to get sick and that mint could help an upset stomach. "They can use the herbs for tea too."

She focused on Cyrus. "I's. . . I'll be at the rooming house or at the bakery over the next few days."

Cyrus nodded. "Good. I'll be sure to come fetch you as soon as they arrive so that you can assist them." He gave them another nod before making his way toward another church member.

"I hope the runaways make it. I've been praying about them whenever I think about them," Joseph commented.

Ruth nodded. "Me too. I really want to help them find freedom." She also wanted to tell them about her own journey from Maryland to Philadelphia. Of course, she was not an escaped slave, but she had a lot to share about how she'd made a new life for herself, getting paid to bake bread and helping the abolitionists.

Joseph touched her elbow. "Ruth, before we were interrupted by Cyrus, I was about to ask you something."

"Yes?"

"May I walk you to your rooming house?" He balled his hands into fists, and his light brown skin reddened. He looked nervous, nervous as a schoolboy. What in the world did he want to speak with her about?

7

Joseph eyed the food-laden table. He'd successfully transformed the bakery into a nice dining space for himself and Ruth. The crude wooden table had a cloth laid over it.

He'd closed the shutters on the windows so the early evening light wouldn't shine on them.

He needed total privacy this evening. The only other person who knew about his private supper with Ruth was Cyrus. He'd wanted Cyrus to know where to find him and Ruth if the runaways arrived this evening. He'd also confided to the elderly pastor about his feelings for Ruth, and Cyrus had encouraged him to make his feelings known to her. If Ruth shared his feelings, then he knew they had a rocky road in front of them. Once Mother found out how he felt about Ruth, she'd have a fit. He could imagine her bony shoulders shaking with rage when he made his intentions known to her.

He lit the candles and eyed the chicken and ham he'd prepared as soon as Mother had left for the day. She had a charity meeting to attend, and he imagined Francine would be there too. He could imagine Francine speaking with Mother, upset that he'd not asked her to the charity ball. He closed his eyes and imagined Ruth in a fancy dress. Her dark hair would be uncovered, and he imagined her loose curls would dangle down her slim back. She was so pretty, he didn't think she needed the face paint that some women used. She looked perfect just the way she was.

After the abolitionist meeting the previous evening, he'd escorted Ruth to her rooming house. He asked her to supper, and she surprisingly agreed. His request had startled her. He could tell by the way her eyes widened.

Well, he was tired of hiding his feelings, and now it was time to do something about it.

A loud knock sounded at the door. He'd locked the door earlier, so he figured it was Ruth. He opened the door and smiled. Ruth sported the dress she'd worn to church last Sunday. She also wore a fancy bonnet; it was red, and a pattern of flowers decorated the headpiece. She clutched her battered reticule as if she were nervous. He finally found his voice. "Ruth, so glad to see you. Come in." He took her hand and guided her into the room.

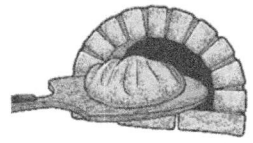

Ruth's hand warmed as Joseph led her into the bakery. Her mouth dropped open when she spotted the fancy meal. Candles flickered in the semidarkness. She blinked, her mind spinning. Well, when Joseph asked her to come to supper, she wasn't sure what to expect. She'd spoken with Miss Tilley after the abolitionist meeting the previous night. The schoolmarm had advised her to speak with Joseph and tell him the truth about her background. "There's no need to keep secrets from him any longer." The older woman had then reminded her that the only reason she'd initially told her to keep her background a secret was because she was concerned about Elizabeth Adams's reaction.

Joseph's mother could be quite intimidating, that was for sure. But Ruth could handle her. But she honestly didn't know if she could handle the growing attraction between herself and Joseph. "This. . .looks so nice, Joseph." She still struggled to use proper speech, but Miss Tilley had been great with her lessons. She'd advised her to think before she spoke, giving her time to recall the rules of English. Thinking first proved tiresome, but she'd been improving, and that was the important thing.

"Thank you, Ruth. Come and sit down." He led her to the table and helped her into a chair. He sat across from her, still holding her hand. He bowed his head. "Lord, thank You so much for Ruth's company tonight. Please allow me to open my mouth and say the right words to her. Please also be with us as we share this meal together. Please, Lord, be with me as I continue to work toward my pastoral endeavors. And Lord, please be with the runaways as they make their journey to Philadelphia. Amen."

Ruth squeezed his hand. "Amen." They feasted on flavorful fried chicken, fried ham, flaky biscuits slathered with butter, and fresh peas. Ruth resisted the urge to lick her lips. Miss Tilley had also been teaching her proper table manners, but sometimes Ruth longed to forget those proper etiquette rules and just be herself. Was it possible to be proper about everything as a second nature?

"What's the matter, Ruth? You were frowning." Joseph gathered their dirty dishes.

She ignored his question. "You. . . Do you need help with the dishes?" She figured he was going to take them back to the kitchen to wash them.

He stopped gathering their dishes. "No, I want to know what you were thinking a few seconds ago."

She inwardly winced. She'd come to tell him the truth about herself, so maybe this was a great time to start.

"Why don't we have dessert before you tell me what's on your mind."

Oh, so he had dessert too? He abandoned their table and went behind the counter. He returned with a yellow cake. A thin glaze was drizzled over the top of the confection, and cherries decorated the top. He sliced two generous pieces and plopped them onto their plates. She wanted to eat the cake with her fingers. Instead, she followed Joseph's lead and sliced into the cake with a fork. The moist, delicate cake melted on her tongue. Sweetness exploded in her mouth.

"Joseph, this is so good. I likes it." She inwardly groaned. In her excitement she'd forgotten about her proper English, but Joseph didn't seem to notice as he ate his cake.

"Thank you."

She was a great bread baker, but cakes were not

something she made very often. Her master only allowed them to bake cake for birthdays and holidays. They each ate two pieces of the wonderful cake. Afterward, Joseph served up some hot coffee with milk and sugar.

"So why were you frowning a few minutes ago?"

Could she open herself up and be completely honest with him? She sighed and looked into his hazel eyes. The candles flickered in the darkness, and she figured she needed to be honest with him. Joseph had been kind to her. She realized she actually trusted him. She took a deep breath. "I's. . . I was thinking about the table manners Miss Tilley has been teaching me. Your food was so good, I wanted to eat it with my fingers."

He laughed. The loud, wonderful sound filled the small bakery. His eyes twinkled as he looked at her. "I understand. Mother still chastises me about eating fast, and I'm a grown man."

Ruth nodded.

He took her hand. "So why has Miss Tilley been teaching you table manners?"

"I wanted to learn to read, write, and speak proper. She been teaching me table manners too."

He raised his eyebrows. Thankfully, he didn't interrupt her. "Joseph, I was a slave. My master set me free when he died." He squeezed her hand, as if encouraging her to continue. She told him all about her master's death and her journey from Maryland to Philadelphia with the help of the abolitionists. She mentioned how Cyrus helped her to find the job at the bakery, and she also told him about Thomas's untimely death. "Joseph, I was in love with Thomas. I still am... I still dream about him. I sometimes think the Lord wants me to be unmarried for the rest of my life and help other people escape slavery."

He frowned, and his hazel eyes no longer sparkled, but he continued holding her hand. "Ruth, you can't—"

A loud banging on the door shattered the silence. Joseph dropped her hand and rushed to the door. He unlocked it and opened it. Cyrus Brown stood at the door, his balding head shining amid the streetlamps. Leaning on his cane, he poked his head into the bakery and spoke to both of them. "The escaped slaves are here. We need your help."

Ruth blew out the candles and joined Cyrus and Joseph at the door. Looked like it was going to be a long night.

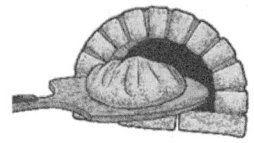

Joseph opened the door to the secret room underneath the church. Ruth eyed the five occupants. A tall, lanky white man was laid out on a pallet in the corner, snoring. She assumed he was the conductor.

Two boys, both looking to be around ten years old. A man and a woman. The couple held hands and the woman rubbed her stomach. They sat on the pallets on the floor and leaned against the wall.

They guzzled water from tin cups. Ruth narrowed her eyes, unsure of how hard their journey was. "Don't drink too fast," she advised them. She feared if they drank a lot of water too quickly, they might get sick.

They nodded, and she poured more water for them. They sipped it and then nibbled on bread, their dark eyes tired. She and Joseph and Cyrus ministered to the runaways for an hour before more church members arrived. The church members agreed to stay with the runaways so that Joseph and Ruth could leave.

"I'll be back tomorrow," she commented. Ruth wanted to tell the runaways about her experiences in a new place, and she hoped she could provide some guidance for them. She also needed to bring the herbs Cyrus had requested. The runaways were supposed to stay for a few days before continuing their journey toward Canada.

Before she and Joseph left, they joined hands with Cyrus and the other church members. They formed a circle around the slaves and the sleeping conductor. They bowed their heads. Joseph cleared his throat. "Lord, we come before You today to seek help. We want to help these people escape to Canada. Please let Your Holy Spirit guide them. Please protect them and help them to stay strong and healthy during their journey. Amen." His voice boomed throughout the room and the sleeping conductor opened his eyes for a few seconds before falling back to sleep.

Joseph touched each of the runaways before he led Ruth out of the church. Her heart skipped when he held her hand as they made their way toward the street. Fatigue weighed upon her like a ton of bricks, and she sighed. *Lord, please help me to get a good sleep tonight. I don't want Elizabeth to get angry with me when I can't stay awake to bake the bread tomorrow.*

"Joseph!" Elizabeth's stern voice pierced the dark night, causing Ruth's heart to thud.

She rushed toward them, her mouth pressed tightly, and her bony shoulders shook with apparent rage. She glared at their joined hands. "What is the meaning of this?"

They'd barely left the church when Joseph's ma appeared. How had she found them? "Mother, what do you want?"

"I saw Francine at the charity meeting, and she told me about the church where you've been worshipping. She claims you're involved in the abolitionist movement. Is that true?"

"Mother, we can talk about this later. I—"

Elizabeth screeched, tears coursing down her cheeks as she again eyed their joined hands. She rushed away.

"Joseph, you need to go after your ma."

"But I want to be sure you get home."

She gestured down the street. "I's be okay."

He shook his head. "I've only seen Mother this angry once in my life. You cannot talk to her about anything when she's so upset. I must wait until later to speak with her."

Ruth disagreed—he needed to go after his ma. She chewed her lower lip as he held her hand while escorting her to the rooming house.

He then pressed his lips against her forehead. "After we get some rest, we need to finish the conversation we started earlier."

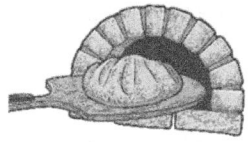

Unable to sleep, Ruth arrived at the church a few hours before her workday started. She knocked on the door, and a church member answered and led her to the hidden stairs behind the church. They walked down the steps, and Ruth pushed the door open, entering the secret room. Surprisingly, the couple was awake, but the boys and the conductor were sleeping. She nodded toward the couple who were sitting up on their pallets. "Hello, I didn't get a chance to introduce myself earlier. My name is Ruth."

"Hello, Ruth." The man greeted her and introduced himself and his wife. His wife rubbed her belly. "I's two months pregnant," she announced.

Ruth raised her eyebrows. She'd heard that pregnant women usually could not make the trip because it was too difficult for them. She figured since this woman was only two months pregnant, she wasn't as fragile as a woman who was further along with a pregnancy.

"I hope your baby is born free. I have faith it will happen."

The woman bopped her head. "Thank you."

She removed her herbs, and over the next hour, she showed them the different herbs she was providing to them. She told them to sniff each one so that they could identify them. "Drink the echinacea each day as a tea. If you can't find water, then chew it. It'll help you to stay healthy." Once she was finished telling about the herbs, she focused on telling them about her life. "I just want you to know how the Lord has guided me from Maryland to Philadelphia as a manumitted slave. I work now and receive wages, and I want you to know that it's possible for you to get a job too. I prayed for this every day, and I wants you to pray for freedom and hope for a better life." She took a deep breath as she began telling them about the events that led up to her journeying to Philadelphia.

8

Two days. Joseph didn't know if he could last another day like this. Mother had not spoken to him, not one word, since she'd found him holding Ruth's hand.

The Baker's Bride

He was also worried about his sermon. Tomorrow he'd be presenting his sermon to the church, and his stomach had been tied up in terrible knots.

He'd been fasting, asking the Lord for guidance regarding his mother's attitude, his feelings for Ruth, and his sermon. He'd noticed Ruth's dark eyes on him, as if she were questioning his silence. He figured she'd say something when she was ready. They'd never finished their conversation they'd started during their special supper. He just found everything so overwhelming. He couldn't focus on his mother's caustic attitude, his feelings for Ruth, and his sermon at the same time. So, he decided he needed to concentrate solely on his sermon for now.

He'd been happy to discover the runaways had left late last night for their next stop. He continued to pray for them whenever they crossed his mind. Lord, please help them to find freedom.

As he put out the fire at the end of the workday, Ruth approached him. "Joseph? You okay?"

He took her hand. "No." He lowered his voice. "I've never seen Mother so angry for such a long time."

"She is upset. I can tell." Pausing, she stared at him for a few seconds. "Your sermon is tomorrow, right?"

He nodded.

"I've been praying for you. I hope you do well."

He nodded and hugged her. "Thank you, Ruth." He studied her as she left, still recalling they needed to sit down and talk. Well, after his sermon was over, and after Mother cooled down, then he'd speak with Ruth. He pulled out his pocket watch. Mother would probably be leaving to go home soon. Well, he didn't want to delay speaking with her any longer.

He knocked on her office door. "Mother. I need to speak with you."

Even though she didn't respond, he opened the door. Surprisingly, she wasn't going over the numbers. She sat in her chair and stared out the window. Tears coursed down her sunken cheeks. He pressed his handkerchief into her hands. "Mother, when was the last time you've eaten?"

She shrugged, refusing to look at him. Mother could be so impossible when she got into one of her moods. He went up front and found a few pieces of Ruth's bread. He buttered them and poured a large cup of water. He returned with the small meal. "Eat, Mother. Then we can speak about what's troubling you."

She stared at the plate for a long time, almost as if she'd never seen a plate of bread before. She then bit into the bread and sipped the water. Once she'd finished eating, he closed the shutter on the window and sat on a chair in front of her. "Mother, my affections for Ruth should not upset you like this."

"Affections?" She spat the word as if it left a bad taste in her mouth. "I saw you looking at that dreadful girl when she first came into our bakery. I never should have hired her. I'm firing her on Monday."

His heart skipped, and he narrowed his eyes. "No, you aren't. Mother, I know how much you love money. Our coffers have greatly increased since Ruth's employ. Father would be ashamed of you right now."

Her mouth dropped open. "Don't talk to me about your father."

"Mother, we must talk about Father. You've not been yourself since he died. You don't eat half the time. You cry every night. I know you miss Father, and you are sad, but don't let your sour attitude cloud your judgment."

He closed his eyes. *Lord, help me to say the right words.* "Even if you were to fire Ruth, it won't solve anything. I'm going to ask Ruth to court me."

"No." Her voice echoed in the small room.

"Mother, is this what you want? To be alone?"

"What do you mean?"

"I hate working in our bakery. I'd be happier if I never baked another loaf of bread in my life."

She pressed her bony hands together, sobbing. "Joseph. . ."

"I want to be pastor at my new church." He then explained that Cyrus was retiring. "If they like my sermon, I may be voted into the pastorship, Lord willing."

She shook her head, the red kerchief on her head bopping. "Joseph, you are not thinking clearly. That girl put these horrid ideas in your head. She told you to become a pastor. I'll bet she even convinced you to join the abolitionist movement."

"That girl has a name, Mother. It's Ruth, and you'd better learn to say it. As far as the movement, I joined myself. I feel called to help others find freedom. I started doing this shortly before I met Ruth." He paused and licked his lips. "I felt unfulfilled at our old church, so I joined another and became involved in the movement."

"Son, just give them some money for the cause. You can help that way."

"Mother, no."

She grabbed his hand, tears streaming from her eyes. "I hear that kind of work is dangerous. What if a slave catcher comes and pulls a weapon on you while you're helping those runaways? Son, I've already lost your daddy. I don't want to lose you too."

His heart thumped as he pulled his mother into his arms. "Mother, I'm sorry." He'd never stopped to think how this would affect her. Mother always wanted to act tough and in control. Well, she needed to understand she couldn't control everything. "I promise I'll be careful." He released her. Hopefully, she wasn't still angry. He may as well be honest with her about everything. He was tired of hiding things from her, hoping to keep her from one of her moods. "I want to help people. I was talking to Cyrus about this the other day, and he said I was already pastoring and did not know it."

She frowned. "You were talking to Cyrus about what?"

He sighed. "Pastoring. When you make your trips to the bank each week, I let some beggars into the bakery. I feed them, but I also talk to them about the Bible and salvation. Mother, they have questions, and I can't answer them all, but I want them to know that God is watching out for them. I want them to have faith. Can you understand that?"

She gasped. "You've been letting homeless bums into our bakery? Do the customers see them?" She actually looked as if she were in pain and was about to cry again.

"I take them into the back."

"Into this office?" She screeched the words as if she were having a fit.

"No, Mother, into the room where we keep our extra supplies."

Well, he didn't want to upset her further. He feared she might faint if she realized how much bread and milk he gave away each week.

"Son, if I can't change your mind about the movement and pastoring, then please listen to my reasoning about Ruth. She'll never fit into our world. She's not the right woman for you. She's poor, and she talks like an uneducated slave."

"Because she was a slave."

She cried again. "Oh my. . .she was a slave?" Her

hands shook, and Joseph rushed to get her more water.

"Mother, calm down. Don't make yourself sick with worry."

She dropped the cup of water and it spilled onto the floor. Joseph mopped up the mess with a towel. "Ruth's a manumitted slave. She's free now and is trying to make a fresh start. Your negative attitude toward her is not helpful. Ruth is a sweet, lovely, God-fearing girl, and you'd see that if you'd just give her a chance." It proved galling and embarrassing that his mother would not learn to accept Ruth.

"But Joseph. What about Francine? She's more your type of girl. Just give her a chance.

She's beautiful, rich, upper-class. . ."

"Mother, I can't control my feelings. I don't love Francine." There was something about Francine that bothered him. He didn't trust her, and the thought of spending more time with her made him uneasy.

"Oh, you love that dreadful girl Ruth?"

He gritted his teeth. No way could he continue to speak with Mother when she was like this. Besides, he needed to go over his sermon a few more times before he spoke to the church tomorrow. He turned and left the office.

The Baker's Bride

Ruth sat in the front pew of the church. She'd gotten up early, wanting to make sure she got a seat in the front so that she could hear Joseph. Miss Tilley had still been eating breakfast when Ruth left for the church. Ruth had been too nervous to eat. She'd been up half the night, praying Joseph's sermon would make an impact on the congregation.

She'd also spent the night thinking about their supper that had been interrupted right after the runaways arrived. Since they'd assisted the runaways, Joseph had been so quiet. He'd seemed like he had a lot on his mind, and she knew he had a lot to handle with his mother's moodiness as well as preparing his sermon. Miss Tilley had encouraged her to speak with Joseph tomorrow. If his sermon was well accepted by the congregation, then he might be in a better mood to talk.

Heaven help her, she was still unsure about Joseph's feelings toward her. Sure, they'd shared a candlelit supper, but she still had Thomas on her mind. However, she finally admitted to herself that her thoughts of Thomas weren't as strong since she'd become involved with the abolitionist movement and had spent more time with Joseph. She found herself admiring Joseph so often, craving his company.

Were these feelings about Joseph God's way of nudging her to see that she may not want to be alone for the rest of her life?

The murmuring from the crowd snapped into her thoughts. She gazed around the sea of folks who were waiting to hear Joseph speak. She scanned the crowd and didn't spot Elizabeth. She hoped Joseph had finally told his mom about his pastoral endeavors. However, if he did tell his mother about his plans, she could imagine Elizabeth not supporting her son. She'd probably be distressed and refuse to hear Joseph preach.

What a rough life, living with Elizabeth Adams.

Ruth smiled when Joseph walked up to the podium. He looked so handsome in his brown suit and polished shoes. He clutched his black Bible in his large hands. He placed it on the podium and then looked directly into the audience. He looked directly at her. His hazel eyes sparkled as he gave her a small, nervous smile. "Good morning," he greeted them.

"Good morning."

"Let's start with a word of prayer." He paused for a few seconds. "Lord, please be with me as I deliver the first sermon of my life. Please open up the ears of this congregation; allow them to understand my words. Help them to find spiritual guidance from my sermon. Please, Lord, continue to be with the runaways as they travel to Canada. Please allow them to arrive safely at their destination. Amen."

"Amen," the congregation murmured.

"Most of you know that I'm a baker. I recently lost my father, and I run the bakery with my mother. Every day we bake bread, and that bread brings sustenance to all those who purchase it. They may eat it for breakfast, dinner, or supper. Well, after you eat that bread, you're going to get hungry again. But God's Word is just like that bread. . .except it's bread from which we'll never grow hungry again." He lifted his Bible and flipped the pages. "Please turn with me to. . ."

Ruth listened, transfixed by Joseph's strong, confident voice. He continued his moving sermon. Once he was finished, the entire congregation clapped. Ruth scanned the crowd, noticing some of the church members cried, their brown cheeks stained with salty tears.

Joseph smiled before bowing his head and closing with another prayer.

Ruth grinned. She ached to go up to the podium and tell Joseph just how proud she was that he'd written such a moving sermon. The congregation had barely started to leave when Francine strolled into the sanctuary. She wore a yellow dress, and her dark curls bounced against the fabric. "Joseph." She cooed his name as if she were a bird calling out to her mate.

His light brown skin reddened as he turned toward

Francine. The rest of the congregation stopped and stared—Francine proved a beautiful sight. She looked so glorious that Ruth could imagine the men aching to stare at her all day.

"Joseph." She spoke his name again, and he appeared speechless as he patiently stood at the podium. Francine soon stood beside him. She then looked out at the audience, toying with his lapel. "You can't go without announcing our betrothal to your church." She then kissed him on the mouth.

Ruth's heart sped up, and she rushed from the church. She heard Miss Tilley's voice over the drone of the audience, calling out to her, but she just couldn't stay. Tears of shame rushed down her face.

9

Joseph banged on the door. The door squeaked as it was swung open. Miss Tilley's eyes widened behind her spectacles. "Joseph. You were just here an hour ago."

"Ruth still isn't here?"

"No. I already told you if she showed up that I'd let her know you were here."

But if Miss Tilley told Ruth he'd been here, that still wouldn't make things better. He needed to talk to her. He didn't want to wait until tomorrow when she showed up to work at the bakery. It'd been two hours since Francine had pulled that terrible shenanigan. "Miss Tilley, you've known me for a long time. You know I am not engaged to Francine. That woman is nothing but trouble, and she fabricated that whole encounter this morning." He wouldn't be surprised if Mother had schemed with Francine too. After he'd unsuccessfully tried to find Ruth, he'd gone to his house. Mother had not been there. Her absence proved disturbing since she always rushed home after church for Sunday dinner. He had to wonder if Mother was with Francine right now, trying to come up with another scheme to hurt Ruth.

Miss Tilley touched his arm. "I know you're not engaged to Francine, but now you've got to convince Ruth." She paused and leaned against the doorframe. "You know, since you were here earlier, I've been thinking. . ."

"Yes?" He'd take any advice he could get. All he wanted to do was fix things with Ruth.

"Ruth once told me she'll sometimes go for a walk in Fairmount Park on Sunday afternoons. You might find her there." She threw her hands up in the air. "I apologize for not thinking about this earlier. But—"

He patted her shoulder. "Thank you. Don't apologize. I'm grateful for your help." He rushed down the steps. He needed to get there as soon as possible. His Sunday shoes clomped against the cobbled street as he rushed toward the park. Sweat beaded on his forehead and rolled down his face. He could imagine Mother's reprimands about his running down the street on a Sunday afternoon. Mother needed to realize protocol was not always relative to the situation at hand. Sometimes, when you needed to get something done, you must do all that was within your power to make it happen, even if you broke a few social rules. Winded, he rounded the corner and approached the park. *Lord, I need Your help. Please help Ruth to understand she doesn't need to live her life alone. Please, Lord, be with her as she listens to what I have to say.*

He rushed into the park. Flowers bloomed and the sun shone on the bright green grass. He slowed to a walk as soon as he spotted Ruth. She sat on a bench, staring up at the sky. The breeze blew, and the leaves of the maple tree danced in the warm spring breeze. He focused on Ruth, and she looked toward him. Their eyes locked like two pieces of a puzzle. "Ruth, please don't run away."

Thankfully, she stayed right on the park bench. Good. Now all he needed to do was rectify everything. He approached the bench and noticed Ruth's red eyes and tearstained cheeks. Well, looked like he had some explaining to do. Now they could continue the conversation they'd started days ago.

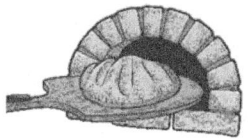

Ruth eyed Joseph as he plopped onto the bench beside her. He'd obviously been running. Sweat clung to his face, and she noticed his strong, muscular arms beneath his sweaty shirt. His mouth mashed down as if he were angry. Well, he'd told her not to run away, so she wouldn't. She'd listen to his words.

"Ruth, I'm sorry." He reached over as if he wanted to take her hand, but then he pulled his hand back.

She figured he didn't want to make her angry. Well, she was mighty angry, so angry she didn't know what to say.

"I'm not engaged to Francine."

"She kissed you."

"I didn't return her kiss. I didn't even know she was coming to our church today. She worships at Mother's church. I think Francine and Mother came up with a plan to make you upset." He touched her face.

She sensed the aftermath of her tears had dried onto her skin, and she probably looked frightful.

"Looks like they succeeded. . .making you upset. I hate seeing you cry, Ruth."

This whole conversation made no sense. "Why would your ma and Francine want to upset me?"

He reached for her hand, and this time he took it. He cradled it in his large palm and kissed each of her fingers. "I like you, Ruth. When I made supper for you, I did that because I wanted to ask if I could court you. I never got around to asking because the escaped slaves arrived. Then Mother was in one of her moods. I told her I wanted to court you, and she got upset." He paused and took a deep breath.

Joseph looked so tired and tormented. The circles beneath his eyes and the droop to his comely lips made her realize just how many troubles he carried on his broad shoulders.

"Mother mentioned Francine would be a perfect mate for me. I got mad. I think Mother wanted to make me change my mind about Francine. That's why I believe she sent Francine to the church today, just to make you jealous."

Goodness, he really wanted to court her? In spite of his mother's objections and his social standing, he still wanted to court her, a former slave? But could she really let Joseph court her? She liked him too, but she didn't know if she wanted to have anybody court her now, or ever. "Joseph, I like you too."

He grinned. "I'm glad to hear that, Ruth."

"But remember what I told you when we shared supper?"

"You feel called to help people escape slavery. You

don't want to be attached to anybody. You were in love with Thomas, and you still think about him."

Well, that was a blessing. He was a man who listened. He'd heard all she'd revealed to him that day. She considered herself to be a strong, courageous woman, a woman who was destined to be alone, doing good for others. But she couldn't deny the feelings she'd developed for Joseph Adams over the last few weeks. "I don't know what to say."

"Would you like some time to think about it?"

She nodded. She figured she'd be spending the next few days praying, hoping the Lord would see fit to show her what to do.

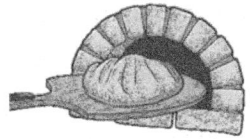

The soft classical music drifted from the closed front door of Joseph's home. If memory served him correctly, it sounded like Mozart. He frowned as he slowly opened the door. He softly closed it and placed the antislavery notices he'd recently picked up from the printers on the hallway table. He then quietly followed the sound of the music. He spotted Mother in the sitting room, her back toward him, playing a flute. She finished playing the classical song. She sniffed. "I didn't realize you'd be home so soon." She placed the flute onto a nearby table and turned toward him. Her face was wet, but she no longer seemed angry. She just seemed sad, and her shoulders drooped. Looked like she was tired too.

He slowly approached her. His mind stirred with so many questions. Confusion filled his soul as he dropped onto a chair beside her. He offered her his handkerchief. "Mother? You can play the flute?" In his entire life, he'd never known her to play anything. He didn't even realize she enjoyed music.

She slowly nodded, wiping her face. "I used to play a long time ago. After I married your father and became involved with the bakery, and had you. . .time just got away from me, I guess."

Well, that didn't explain much. Why would getting married and having a baby make her want to stop playing the flute? He needed to understand what was going on with her. "Why are you playing now?"

She shrugged. "I guess I'm just so sad about you not taking a liking to Francine. Everything I've been working so hard for is just ruined. Playing used to help me escape from my problems. Decided to try it again now, I guess."

"Why do you say everything is ruined? I don't understand."

"Son, when I married your father. . .well, we wanted to start a family."

He nodded. He still had tons of questions he wanted to ask her but sensed he needed to let her open up to him when she was ready.

"You're not my firstborn. I had two other children before I had you."

His heart stilled. "What?"

"You heard me. I had two children before you. Both of them died when they were infants. Then I had you. You were sick as a baby but you survived. Son, I've always been so proud of you. You're charming, good-looking, compassionate, sometimes too compassionate. Before your father died, I promised him I'd help you find the perfect wife. Both of us felt Francine would be a perfect match."

"Mother, I've explained—"

She touched his hand. "I know. I've just been so focused on doing what I and your father felt was right for you that I haven't been paying attention to how my actions have affected you. Son, I just didn't want to further alienate you. I don't want to lose you."

"Mother, you will never lose me. I will always love you and be your son." He took her hand and squeezed it. "Is there anything else you want to tell me?"

She nodded. "I have to be honest with you. I schemed with Francine. I agreed to her meeting you at the church and kissing you. You're so smart you probably figured that out on your own."

He nodded, still holding her hand. "Yes. Mother, you hurt Ruth. I like her. I honestly don't know if she'll agree to court me, but even if she doesn't, I know that there's no future between me and Francine.

I can't be with a woman I can't trust."

"I'm sorry, Son. I really am. I now realize I took things too far, and for that I'm truly sorry."

He nodded. "I forgive you." A miracle had just occurred. He couldn't believe that Mother had actually admitted she'd been wrong. Well, he needed to tell her something that might make her feel better. "I like hearing you play. You should do it more often."

She actually smiled. He then abandoned his seat and made a pot of coffee. He spent the entire evening talking to his mother, asking her questions, hoping that he could help erase the rift that had grown between them.

Ruth lay on her bed and stared at the ceiling of her bedroom. It'd been two days since Joseph's question about courting her. A loud knock on the door interrupted her thoughts. "Come in."

Miss Tilley came into the room. She pushed her glasses up on her nose. "Have you been all right?"

Miss Tilley seemed to be able to know when something was bothering her. She may as well be truthful. "No."

"Your mind has been wandering the last couple of

days during our school lessons." The older woman pulled her chair up to the bed and took a seat. She patted Ruth's leg. "You've made excellent progress on your lessons. Your speech has improved."

"Thank you, Miss Tilley." She'd even started reading some of the simple children's nursery rhyme books. She'd been working hard on learning her letters, and she figured in due time, Mrs. Adams might let her wait on the customers in the bakery. The woman barely paid her any attention. She often wondered if Mrs. Adams noticed her speech had improved since she'd been hired to work in the bakery.

Miss Tilley cleared her throat. "I worked with Joseph this evening."

"You did?" This was surprising. She didn't realize Miss Tilley would be helping Joseph.

"Yes. I helped him to hang some antislavery notices. We're trying to get some more people to come to our next abolitionist meeting. We're expecting some more runaways in a couple of weeks."

She'd known Joseph was going to be hanging notices, but she didn't realize he'd be doing that this evening. Normally, she would have assisted him with the task, but she'd seen him all day at the bakery. She needed some time away from him to think about his offer of courtship.

"How are things going at the bakery?"

"I's. . . I've been working hard like usual."

"Are you getting along with Mrs. Adams?"

She resisted the urge to roll her eyes. "She don't. . .doesn't talk to me, Miss Tilley. She doesn't look at me. Only reason I'm still there is because of my bread. The profits are good, so she tolerates me."

"How about Joseph? He was mighty upset about what happened last Sunday with Francine. He told me you two talked at the park."

"Yes, we talked." She then told Miss Tilley about Joseph wanting to court her. "I don't know if I should let him court me. I wonder if I'd be happier by myself."

"Have you prayed about it?"

"Yes, a lot."

"What do you feel in here?" Miss Tilley touched her chest. "In your heart?"

"I like Joseph. It made me mad when Francine kissed him. I hated seeing her around him when we were passing out the pamphlets earlier this month."

"Are you still sad about Thomas?"

"Not as much since I've started working in the bakery. I still dream about him, think about him."

Miss Tilley nodded. "Grief can be like that sometimes. When my pa died, it was awful. Took me a while to get used to his being gone. I still think about him a lot."

Ruth nodded. "Sorry about your pa."

She waved her hand. "It happened a long time ago. Now, tell me how you feel about Joseph."

"I like Joseph. He's kind, honest, and trusting. I like

how he helps people."

"Are you referring to his helping with the abolitionist movement?"

"Yes, but I'm also talking about his helping people in the city. He feeds homeless people and tells them about the Bible. He really cares, and seeing him care for folks like that, feeding them, wanting to nourish their souls"—she swallowed and continued to gather her thoughts—"makes me feel happy in here." She pressed her hand to her chest. "My heart gets glad just seeing him minister. Plus, he's handsome. I could sit and look at him all day."

Miss Tilley grinned. "I think you know what you need to do, Ruth."

She frowned. "I do?"

"What would Thomas want you to do? Do you think he'd want you to be alone for the rest of your life?"

She'd never thought of it like that. She knew Thomas would want her to be happy. "Ruth, from hearing you speak, you want to spend time with Joseph and get to know him better, but you are scared of being hurt again." She took Ruth's hand and squeezed her fingers. "Don't be afraid to love again. The Lord wants you to be happy, and if being with Joseph brings you happiness, then you should let him court you." Miss Tilley hugged her then left the room and closed the door behind her.

Joseph pulled out a chair for Ruth. They'd just closed the bakery, and Mother had already gone home. Mother was still strangely silent during the workday, clearly unsettled about his affections for Ruth. She still didn't speak to Ruth, but at least she no longer glared at her like she used to. Ever since she'd told him about her deceased children and her aspirations for him as her only living child, it was like a barrier had been removed from between them. For the last couple of nights, they'd shared coffee and had a decent conversation. He was finding things out about his mother he'd never known, and he'd encouraged her to consider playing the flute as worship to God.

He eyed Ruth as she sat in her seat. Earlier, she'd requested to speak with him after closing, and he'd gladly agreed. *Lord, please let Ruth agree to my courtship.*

She removed her bonnet and he admired the bunch of curls gathered on her head. He sat beside her as she pulled her dinner pail from the floor. She reached into the pail and removed a small wrapped parcel. "This is for you." Her dainty hands shook as she gave him the package. She looked nervous. Well, he was nervous too.

He studied the package before untying the knotted twine. Two heart-shaped sugar cookies were nestled within the folds of paper. "You baked these for me?"

She nodded. "I's... I like you, Joseph. I baked these for you to let you know that my answer is yes. I want you to court me."

He grinned and pulled Ruth into his arms. She smelled like vanilla and cinnamon. He took her soft, dainty hand and squeezed her fingers. He bit into the thin confection, and the taste of sugar and vanilla exploded in his mouth with delicate sweetness. He offered the cookie to Ruth and she took a small bite.

He then leaned toward her and kissed her beautiful lips.

Epilogue

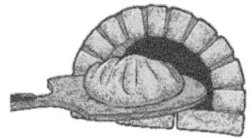

One year later…

Joseph strolled to the podium, holding his Bible. He relished his role as pastor of his church. He'd been the pastor for almost a year, and he was still amazed he'd been chosen to replace Cyrus

Brown. He scanned the audience, his eyes resting on Ruth. She sat in the front seat, her hands resting on her large pregnant stomach. Mother sat right beside her. It had been a rocky road getting the two of them to get along.

After he'd asked Ruth for courtship, they'd spent time together for a month before Cyrus Brown married them. Mother had attended their wedding, and she openly admitted to him beforehand that it was still hard for her to accept Ruth into their lives, but she was willing to try. When he'd started his pastorship, Mother and Ruth began to run the bakery together. Ruth started talking to Mother about more improvements in the bakery. She'd suggested having a cookie day, a day when the bakery sold cookies in addition to their breads and pastries.

Their profits had increased even more, and Mother had finally started to respect Ruth. Now, they ran the bakery together, and Mother had finally started coming to their church. She'd even played her flute for the congregation a few times and had received a lot of compliments about her talent. They'd also hired a new assistant for the bakery once he'd become pastor.

He was still active in the abolitionist movement and Ruth continued to assist in the duties. She continued dispensing dried herbs and encouragement to the runaways, and she thrived in her role as a supporter of the Underground Railroad. He scanned the audience before again focusing on Ruth.

"I love you." She silently mouthed the words.

He often daydreamed of what life would be like once their baby was born. He knew Mother would be pleased to have a grandchild on whom to dote.

"I love you too," he mouthed. His beautiful wife then grinned at him, and he returned her smile before he began his sermon.

About Cecelia Dowdy

Cecelia Dowdy is an Amazon bestselling author who lives near Washington DC. She enjoys listening to old tunes with her husband and spending time with her son. Baking is one of her favorite passions. She loves experimenting with bread recipes using her sourdough starter. Serving homemade desserts to friends brings her joy. Her love of baking shines in her romance novels. When she's not in the kitchen, or spending time with her family, she's cooking up delicious faith-filled plots. Fans say reading her tasty novels makes them hungry. Sign up for her newsletter at www.ceceliadowdy.com.

Connect with Cecelia Dowdy

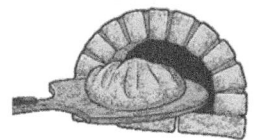

I hope you enjoyed The Baker's Bride.
Join my mailing list for updates about new releases along with fun, inspiring messages: https://ceceliadowdy.com/sign-up-for-my-email-list/

Let's discuss the Bible – visit my Sunday Brunch biblical discussions on my blog: http://ceceliadowdy.com/blog/category/sund

ay-brunch

Please visit my website for more of my books:
www.ceceliadowdy.com/

You can also find me on social media:
www.facebook.com/CeceliaDowdyAuthor/
https://twitter.com/cdnovelist
https://www.bookbub.com/authors/cecelia-dowdy
https://www.tiktok.com/@cdnovelist

Other Titles by Cecelia Dowdy

THE BAKERY ROMANCE SERIES
http://ceceliadowdy.com/bakery-romance-series/

Loving Luke *(Book 0)*
Raspberry Kisses *(Book 1)*
Shades of Chocolate *(Book 2)*
Sweet Dreams *(Book 3)*
Sugar and Spice *(Book 4)*
Southern Comfort *(Book 5)*
Sweet Delights *(Book 6)*
Cinnamon Kisses *(Book 7)*

The Baker's Bride

THE CANDY BEACH SERIES

https://ceceliadowdy.com/the-candy-beach-series2/

Caramel Kisses *(Book 0)*
Chocolate Dreams *(Book 1)*
Milk Chocolate Kisses *(Book 2)*
Bittersweet Dreams *(Book 3)*
Coffee and Kisses *(Book 4)*
Rocky Road Dreams *(Book 5)*

OTHER TITLES

http://ceceliadowdy.com/books/

The Baker's Bride – an Underground Railroad historical novella
The Doctor's Bride – a historical novella

Made in the USA
Coppell, TX
26 February 2024